"We need you for a diversion," said the sheriff.

"You just watch me," Candy said bravely.

She headed toward the door with a firm step. She put her hand on the knob, turned to smile again at the group. Then, in a single burst of courage, she opened the door.

When it slammed behind her, and they heard Candy's steps work their way across the porch, the group returned, kneeling, to the windows. They peered over the sills. Candy was on the lawn. The last few seconds had worked a miraculous change in her and she was no longer a frightened child. Swinging her hips, throwing her shoulders back so that her breasts stood out boldly, she strolled nonchalantly toward the fountain on the right.

"She'll be all right," said Costaign.

Pat looked up, her eyes were red and deepset.

"No, she won't, Bob. None of us will."

THE
ANCIENT
ENEMY

|||||||||||||||||||||||||||||||||||||||||||||||||||||||||||||||||||||||||||||

Donald Thompson

FAWCETT GOLD MEDAL • **NEW YORK**

THE ANCIENT ENEMY

© 1979 Donald Thompson

Published by Fawcett Gold Medal Books, a unit of CBS Publications, the Consumer Publishing Division of CBS Inc.

ISBN: 0-449-14216-7

Printed in the United States of America

10 9 8 7 6 5 4 3 2 1

CHAPTER
ONE

If Dr. Roberto Costaign had taken the south fork of the intersection where Indian Mountain Road meets County 179, he would have swooped down into the low country around Spirit Lake, where the earth levels out, the rocks diminish, and the pine trees throw shadows as cold as refrigerated cream. He would have baited his hooks with worms taken from white sand. His bobber plops would have played alto to the deep organ tones of the wind in the high trees.

Around six, as the sun was setting, he would have scaled and split a couple of wiry trout and fried them in butter over a dry wood fire. Later he would have, unrolled his sleeping bag, stretched out on his back, and relaxed, facing the orange stars while he smoked a fat Prince Albert roll-your-own cigarette. It would have been the perfect first day of a perfect vacation.

As it was, he took the west fork, leading upward to Cherakowa and Lake Campbell. By nightfall, every shred of pride gone, he was screaming to be delivered from a horror he would carry to his grave.

"Good morning," said the voice in the VW dashboard radio. "It's six-fifteen."

The weight on Costaign's eyelids confirmed that much.

"Thirty-nine degrees in KSRH country."

Costaign scrunched down into his blue nylon hunting jacket. He had lived long enough in Las Vegas, so that he no longer noticed the extremes of desert weather, that it would be near freezing before dawn and a hundred and six by noon.

"Here's a reminder from the KSRH Bulletin Board. Beginning Sunday, three days from now, Cherakowa will begin its week-long celebration of the Centennial Fiesta. It'll be the big daddy of the town's famous annual celebrations. Rodeos, carnivals, plenty of food and refreshments, rides for the kids. And—opening day only—1879 prices on everything! Beer: a nickel a glass! Steak dinner with all the trimmings: thirty-five cents! And lots more. Plan to be there. On Wednesday of Fiesta Week, KSRH's Dan Wilson will be on deck with lots of fun, music, and prizes. That's Cherakowa Fiesta Week. Starting this Sunday and lasting the whole week. In Cherakowa. Only eighty miles from Las Vegas. The Old West lives again!"

The instrumental opening of a Merle Haggard record slid underneath the announcer's last five words as he brought the music up.

So that's what all the fuss was about, Costaign thought as the music began. The young doctor had driven through Cherakowa less than ten minutes before. He remembered noting the brightly colored carnival trucks leaning into the roadside like sleeping animals. Well, they could have all that racket and screaming and shoving and kids. Not him. All he wanted was peace. Just a little patch of ground next to Lake Campbell where he could throw up his tent, do some fishing, maybe some reading, and maybe, if a streak of real ambition hit him, a little walking.

Not that his everyday life was so hard. By most standards it was pretty enviable. He was house physician for the Sunburst Hotel on the Vegas Strip, which on one hand, meant a subpenthouse suite, thirty grand a year, the best of food and booze, and access to some of the best-looking chicks in the country. On the other hand, it meant making his "rounds" in the gambling casinos and bars, smiling his Dr. Kildare smile, holding hands with hysterical wives who had not seen their gambling husbands since the night before. It meant gluing junkie starlets back together. It meant hookers and hustlers and shills. It meant patching up a couple of loonies after they'd finished working each other over with knives.

If it wasn't a bad life, it was a pointless life.

Costaign had originally taken the job so he could put together enough money to open his own practice; then the months had just started flying away from him. He guessed it might be fun to let a lot more months fly by, but was this why he had become a doctor? Could he so easily ignore the idealism that had sustained him through med school? Or was he becoming a strange kind of inverse snob? After all, those guests at the Sunburst had as much right to the best medical care they could get as anyone else. Who was he to disapprove of the way they led their lives? Did medical practice only become valid if it were practiced in a ghetto, or the Solomon Islands? He had a feeling he would be doing a lot of self-evaluating this trip.

The road became steeper. Narrower. The flanking, bouldered sides, rising like walls, seemed to have moved in closer. The switchbacks became more frequent, and tighter. Costaign felt the car losing power. Good ol' VW Bug, he thought, zero power going uphill if you are carrying more than a handkerchief in your pocket. He jerked the stick into second and gunned. Hell, these things are supposed to have been made for the Bavarian Alps. Let's go, he coaxed. The Bug responded but very nearly argued before it did. As he approached another switchback, second became feeble. A ram into first, a gulp of gas, and a forward encouraging motion over the wheel sent the car rocketing around the curve.

Then Costaign smashed on the brakes!

He veered into the oncoming lane and rocked to a stop on the far shoulder. The quivering in his stomach attested to the one giddy instant of horror he'd experienced not knowing whether the oncoming lane had been empty.

"Christ!" he said as he squinted at the sight that had caused the sudden stop.

It was a young woman. She was naked. Her blond hair was twisted into unkempt Medusa ropes. When she moved she was as stiff as a puppet: jerky, uncoordinated, off balance. She was raw flesh from head to foot. Her hands flapped at her sides. She would periodically flick them across her body in a vague brushing motion. The expression on her face was the worst of all. Costaign had never seen such terror imprinted on human features. Her lips were wrenched, her eyes bulged, her teeth were bared like those of a skull; tics in her throat and neck throbbed unrestrainedly.

She would stagger a few steps forward. Stop. Then twist her face to heaven. Her hands would absently flick her breasts. Her body would pirouette slowly on its stiff hinges in a weird saraband. Costaign shuddered to imagine the music she must hear to set the beat for such a dance.

"Miss? Miss? Can you hear me? I'm a doctor. Can you tell me what's wrong?" Costaign said, getting out of the car.

He received no answers. No catatonic ever stood more uncomprehendingly as he walked toward her.

He quickly checked over her wounds. As extensive as they were, he saw that they were basically superficial. Nothing that needed immediate attention, but strange, as though the skin had peeled from her as one peels an orange. She stood glowing red in the morning sun. He wrapped her in a lintless thermal blanket which he removed from his sleeping bag. He then folded her into the passenger seat.

"Don't worry," he said to the rigid, unhearing woman, "we'll have you in a nice warm hospital in no time."

Angrily he cranked the VW around and gunned it down toward Cherakowa. Angrily, he thought, who the hell could do this to another human being?

As they drove, the familiar hum of the engine seemed to reach inside the woman and relax her; that, and the warmth of the blanket. Her hands, however, continued their wringing. Her fingers twined and untwined like silent tongues.

"No trouble, Doc. I was up when you called. This damned fiesta's got me run bowlegged. Here. Have some of this. The night shift calls it coffee. It'll put lead in your pencil, if you got anybody to write to."

"No thanks, Sheriff. I've had plenty from my thermos."

Anton Whitney was sheriff of Arapahoe County, of which Cherakowa was the seat. He was a giant. Not much more than five-ten between the floor and the top of his head, but there was a massiveness about him, a suggestion of Cro-Magnon power, as though he could take at least *one* out of three falls against a Kodiak bear.

His physical strength had been, in fact, a matter of legend on the Chicago police force when he had been a cop there. One night he and his partner in their prowl car had received an "Officer Needs Assistance" call and had discovered a brother cop pinned under the rear of his own car. Whitney, not waiting for the assistance that the pinned officer's partner had gone for, had flung himself face down beneath the car next to the pinned man. In one, atomic effort, he had lifted the car so that the other officer could be dragged clear. The mayor had given him a medal. His friends had given him the nickname *Kong*.

His computer eyes and his quick smile suggested the shrewdness of a ward heeler. He had played that game, too, but it was a sore spot with him. He wore his uniform as neatly as a Marine Corps drill instructor.

Settled heavily into his chair, the sheriff felt his forty-eight years. Wake-up paleness was still on his face. His voice was whispery.

"I checked the young blonde in the infirmary before I came here," Whitney said. "There ain't much to tell. She's all scratched up. Her mind is shot. Deep shock. The doc in the infirmary says he don't think she was raped."

"Did he suggest what might have caused the abrasions?"

"Well, no. Not really. Some of them, he said, look like scratches; some others look like cement burns. You know, the kind you'd get if you was riding a bike and you fell off. Course, I don't think she was pedaling no·bike. What do you think might have caused them?" the sheriff asked.

Costaign was about to answer the sheriff's apparently innocuous question until the expression on the big man's face brought him up short.

"Hey, wait a minute, Sherff. You think I'm involved in this, don't you? I resent that. I found her. I didn't put her there. I told the whole story to your sergeant when I brought . . ."

"Don't get your tail in a knot," said the sheriff, waving his paw. "I don't think nothing. I know you're clean."

"That's generous of you. Thanks for taking my word."

Whitney smiled expansively. "I never said I took your word. I'm a cop. And a cop is a guy who gets used to checking things out. After you been on the force for a couple of years, you get so you don't even believe your own family. If you know what I mean. Now there ain't nothing about a medical diploma says you can't break the law. Just like everybody else.

"Sergeant Gomez is a cop, too. So he just naturally checked out everything you told him. You said you were at the Sunburst Hotel till five-fifteen this morning, and that you had been there all night. Gomez thought that was kind of a funny thing for you to say. What with your being a doctor and all, he figured you might be able to tell when the assault occurred. And you might just be coming up with an alibi in advance.

"Our doc figured the assault happened—oh—about sunset last night. So Gomez called the hotel. Your boss says you were there all day yesterday. The night clerk says you left about five this morning. So that clears you. Just for ducks, though, Gomez called your room and who should answer the phone but a Miss—let's see—Miss Kitty Matthews. She says you spent the night with her right from dinner. Says you're crazy for getting out of a warm bed to catch a bunch of slimy fish. Maybe you are. So now we know where you were at sundown last night."

"You did all that since I've been waiting for you?" the young doctor said, with awe in his voice.

"Well, yeah. Cops are like that. So let me ask you again, and this time don't get mad. What do you think happened to the blonde?"

Shaking his head, Costaign relaxed in the chair.

"I can only guess," he said. "I would imagine she got herself mixed up with a couple of sadists and by the time she found out it was too late. You said something interesting a couple of minutes ago about falling off a bike. Maybe she was dragged behind a car or motorcycle."

"Give or take a little, that's about the way I see it," Whitney said. "About the sadists, I mean. Didn't really want to screw her, just wanted to hurt her. One thing bothers me. I'm a guy who likes to keep his eyes open. I want to know who lives in my county—who floats in and out. I got a good memory for faces. Seems to me I've seen that girl before. Unless I'm as blind as a rat's ass, she works up at Eros Ranch. 'Bout a mile from where you found her. Now why would anyone want to treat a whore like that?"

"Whore?"

"Well, sure. Young guy like you—a doctor at the Sunburst Hotel—seems to me you'd know all about that kind of place. Real fancy whorehouse out in the boondocks. Ever since prostitution became legal in this county, I've had four of them "ranches" in my jurisdiction. Nice place to go if you're a tourist. Even better if you're a local guy and you don't want your wife to find out. Be surprised how the sale of fishing gear has gone up since we opened these places."

"So that's where she came from," said Costaign. "I thought she was some poor kid who'd been lured up to the mountains."

"I don't know how much of a poor kid she is, but that ain't no reason for punching the shit out of her. Not in *my* county it ain't. She's trying to make a living, just like the rest of us."

The sheriff stood. He hefted his gun belt.

"Look, Doc, I'm going to take me a ride. How'd you like to come along and show me where exactly you found the blonde? Maybe I'll go to Eros to talk to some people, and you can go about your fishing."

The sun was bright as the two men stepped out into the parking lot. The town of Cherakowa was awake and moving. Cars crawled in and out of the yard as the day shift came on. The sheriff waved to some of the newcomers. He answered a few Hi-yas. The new municipal building, which housed the sheriff's department, was located on the main drag. The doctor and the sheriff, before entering their own cars, watched a convoy of carny trucks rumble by. Costaign noted the banners that spanned the street, brightly directing expected tourists to this concession or that. A streamer fluttered from each light pole. Red, white, and blue litter cans lined the sidewalks.

"Looks like the fiesta is going to be quite a bash," said Costaign.

"It's kind of big to a lot of people. To me it's a pain in the ass."

"That must make you a minority of one. All you can see on the streets are happy faces," said Costaign.

"I don't figure the Indians are too happy. This wingding got started years back as a memorial to a battle between the Indians and the cavalry. Some battle. Cavalry showed up in the middle of the night and killed all the Indians in their sleep. I seen a movie one time when I was a kid about Jim Thorpe. When he was in school some other Indian kid says to him: 'How come, in the history book, whenever whiteman kill Indian, big military victory? When Indian kill whiteman, big massacre?'"

Costaign laughed as he went off to find his own car.

"You go ahead," the sheriff called through his window. "I'll follow."

On the trip back up Indian Mountain Road, the lawman tagged along about a hundred yards behind the VW.

Whitney vaguely envied Costaign. The whole world is that guy's oyster, he thought. Not bad looking: about six feet even, green eyes, dark chestnut hair. Dressed well. He sure didn't buy them hiking boots at no fire sale. He couldn't be more than thirty and look at him already: big deal doctor at the Sunburst. No kicking around the ashcans for that boy. Eats in fancy restaurants every night. Meets famous movie stars in person. Gets all the chorus-girl poontang he could want.

He compared Costaign's life to his own and guessed his hadn't been too much to shout about.

Anton Whitney was born on the high Colorado plains outside Denver. Literally, in a sod hut. Kind of hard to imagine now that they still had them goddam things in 1930, when he was born. His parents had been trying to make a go of a piece of farmland that Jesus H. Christ himself couldn't handle. Always too much work. Never enough of anything else. The thing—of all things—he remembered was the cold. It was high-country cold: lifeless, frigid, paralyzing, like the cold of outer space. He remembered his hands. Trying to work outdoors while the cold made his hands scream with pain. No money for gloves though. Sometimes he worked with rags tied around them, sometimes he didn't. He remembered once, when he was about ten, getting down on his knees in a cloddy field, praying, "Please, God! Give me some gloves right now!" while the wind scalded him through his thin jacket.

When he turned sixteen, he left home. The cold had even begun to penetrate his dreams. He worked in the stock department of May's Department Store for four years in Los Angeles, where it never got cold. At twenty, he joined the army.

The army meant Korea, and the furious damnation of the Pusan Perimeter. The Naktong River countryside had been hilly and rocky, like Colorado, and like Colorado, had its own particular brand of nightmares.

After his discharge, determined to have nothing to do with the West, he accompanied a buddy home to Chicago. From the moment he stepped off the train his life seemed to have a meaning it never had before. Now he had a goal. He took the police exam as soon as it was offered. Four months later, he was a cop. And Dear Jesus! hadn't he seen it all during those first years, on the cruiser patrol! Pimps, whores, junkies, drunks, thieves, muggers, boosters, cutters, killers—the whole shebang.

At age thirty, having buttered up all the right people, he finagled himself into city hall, where he learned to play the political game. For the next ten years things sort of moved along at their own pace. He was Anton Whitney, the farm boy, wearing captain's bars. Not bad. Then one day—bang. Imagine him, like a jerk, getting stuck holding the bag for a shyster like Padney Flaherty.

That was all behind him now. No use raking it up again. He had a good spot here, and he intended to keep it. Being forced to resign from a big city police department when you're forty-four is no joke. He was damned lucky to have what he had. Who knows? There might even be a place to go for a fellow with ambition. State prosecutor maybe. Didn't need a law degree for that here.

The sun had become so bright that Whitney snapped his sunglasses out of the glove compartment. Costaign signaled that they were about to reach the spot where he had discovered the young woman. A hundred yards farther, and they both pulled over.

"You say she was walking when you found her?" Whitney asked. "Seems like the assault might have happened up the road a bit and it took her some time to get where you found her."

They searched the roadsides for signs of struggle, Whitney on one side, Costaign on the other. They found nothing.

"Guess I'd better get poking around Eros. Look, Doc, I'm starting to think that whatever happened, happened at the ranch. For all we know there might be some more people injured. Just in case there are, I'd sure like to have a doctor along. What do you say? Want to give up a few more minutes of your fishing?"

"Sure. I'd be glad to. I don't imagine those fish are going anyplace."

The two cars, the sheriff's now in the lead, worked their way up the road until they reached a dirt cutoff, which was, as Whitney had predicted, just about a half mile from where Costaign had found the woman. Although unpaved, the road was smooth and well cared for. Another two hundred winding yards and the road widened into a tarmac parking lot. The sheriff stopped at the entrance, beeping several times. When no one answered, the two cars pulled into the lot.

The lot, designed for fifty or sixty cars, looked empty with only about fifteen cars parked in it.

"That's funny," the sheriff said as they strolled toward the parked cars. "There's usually a couple of security men on that front gate. Security's real tight up here. Usually you have to get out of your car to be checked out at the entrance, then they park your car while a golf cart takes you up to the main house. Wonder what happened to them security guys."

Costaign accompanied the sheriff as he walked from parked car to parked car, peering inside, running his hand over their hoods.

"Only customers' cars park here," the sheriff continued. "There's a double-deck parking lot fixed right into the main building. That's where the employees park. Ain't that something? Everyone of these cars has been parked here overnight. All these cars got dew on them. The engines are cold. Customers usually go home before this. Let's take a walk up to the house."

The two men cut across the lot toward what Costaign assumed to be the main section of the compound. The sheriff continued talking in his normal manner, but Costaign was sure that he, too, had detected an indefinable strangeness about the place. The sheriff seemed to have subtly changed. His shoulders were hunched forward almost imperceptibly; his eyes had become slits.

Eros Ranch was set in a gigantic gulley that could not properly be called a valley. Its sides were as smooth and round as a teacup. As they walked, the two men could see the red tile roof of the hacienda rise above a large eucalyptus grove before them.

"This place sure smells of something, but I don't know what," the sheriff commented, almost to himself.

Measuring each step, both men walked as though

they were maneuvering in a mine field. They heard no sounds, they saw no movement, saw no people. Only the wind whistled and sighed in the treetops. Costaign felt himself shiver. The pores of his skin seemed to grow sensitive. Sixth sense, he thought. It's real.

The eerie fingers of it caressed his body. It's a built-in warning system. Maybe it was built in when human beings still lived in caves, when every flutter of a bush could maim or kill; where existence was as precarious as a flick or a glance. Let a bush flutter and a switch is thrown. The skin prickles. Adrenalin flows. Eyes and ears become sharper. Muscles tense. The body, as the sheriff's had already, takes on a defensive stance. People in civilized societies rarely get to feel the sixth sense. Soldiers in combat do. So do cops on dark streets, as do firemen in smoldering buildings, and mothers whose chidren are out of sight.

Both the doctor and the sheriff felt it now, but neither spoke of it. The silence became increasingly foreboding as they picked their way through the grove.

A few tense minutes later, they stepped out the other side, onto the main grounds. For just an instant, it seemed, their hearts stopped pumping. Lot's wife never froze more quickly or more solidly than they.

"Jesus Christ," the sheriff whispered and made it sound like a prayer.

The doctor couldn't speak at all.

CHAPTER
TWO

The grounds were a butcher shop. If the Angel of Death had lifted his fist, the judgment would not have been more brutal.

The bodies were male and female. At one time they might have been black or white or brown, but now, in the angled spotlights of morning sun, they oozed crimson. Some lay sprawled on the hacienda's lawn like toppled statues. Some littered the pathways that connected the hacienda with a dozen or so private cottages. Three of the bodies were clustered around a Spanish fountain.

For all that may have separated them in life, all the bodies had a hideous death in common. They could

have been the human scatterings of an airline crash.
Legs were bent or twisted, or angled out in grotesque
attitudes. Arms were frozen upward, as though with
clenched fists they had sought a grip on substantial
air. And the faces. Maddened spheres that had once
been eyes stared out from mushy red flesh, the skull-
bare teeth remained hooked into lips they had tried to
gnaw away!

Death had not been discriminating. Flung out among
the human corpses were several dead rabbits and
prairie dogs. Even a starling lay broken winged and
still. Strangest of all were the insects. Their lifeless
husks lay scattered around, in some areas, as thick as
carpets. Most of the insects were cockroaches, the
inch-and-a-half-long desert variety, which differs from
its smaller, more circumspect urban cousin as a tiger
does from a tomcat. A few locusts and crickets were
mixed in, but it took a sharp eye to spot them. The
husk carpets lay thickest around the fallen human
bodies.

Whitney and Costaign finally took a step forward, a
tentative step. Then another. Then another.

"Jesus Christ," the sheriff whispered again. "We'd
better go see what the inside of the house looks like."

Costaign nodded and wondered where the sheriff got
his courage. Dead roaches crunched under their feet.
Only the constant wind reminded them that there was
still life in the gulley. They mounted the stairs and
clumped across the wide wooden porch, also littered
with dead insects. A circle of rattan chairs sat like a
ghostly reception committee. The main door hung ajar.

The sheriff drew his Magnum. With a single shove of his leg he crashed the door open.

Only silence greeted them inside. The bright sun, filtering through the thick drapes, was a mockery of life. The two men stopped as they reached an old-fashioned parlor that had served as a reception room. The walls were satin flocked. Tulip-bulbed gas lamps, redone for electricity, elbowed out from dark wooden beams. Circular divans and antimacassared armchairs, ankle deep in Persian rugs, were grouped around oval coffee tables.

That fantasy should come to such an end.

The crunching continued underfoot as the two men followed the barrel of the sheriff's gun over a carpet of roach husks.

"No one here," the doctor whispered

"I don't know, but we better stick together."

On the far end of the parlor, opposite the front door, a circular stairway with sweeping banisters curled up to the second floor. They found another body at the base of it.

"Looks like the same thing that happened to that girl on the road happened to these people. What is it, Doc?"

Costaign just shook his head.

"I guess she was lucky. She walked away from it," said the sheriff.

The silence, which outside had been eerie, was terrifying inside. They climbed the stairs, each man enveloped in fearsome tension.

The staircase emptied out into the center of a

maroon-carpeted hallway. Doors opened from both sides of the hall. The sheriff and the doctor moved from room to room, making grisly discoveries. In one room they found a couple. The man was stuffed under the bed, curled fetally. The woman, twisted into a parody of a kneeling position, was propped forward against a wall. In another room, the female half of a couple was curled up in one corner. The man had tried to escape by flinging himself through the glass of a window. He hung, impaled bloodily, on jagged teeth of glass.

The two men moved as though passing through a dreamscape. They touched nothing.

Above all, they were aware of how the inconsistency between what these rooms had been designed for and what had finally occurred in them increased the horror. On one dresser, a lacy bra, its nylon ripped by brute force, rested among the husks of a dozen dead roaches. A lone candle in a silver holder stood alone on a coffee table amid the shambles of what had been a quiet dinner. An overturned wine bottle had spilled its expensive red blood into a rug. A black corselette with red ribbons hung limply over a door knob.

Outside again, the two men systematically poked through the cottages beyond the eucalyptus grove, and through the mobile homes at the base of the gulley wall. The cottages were reserved for customers who had individual fantasies, a sense of the exotic, the romantic, or a desire for privacy. Here, too, death among high, shiny black boots, Victorian corsets, and ball gags. The mobile homes served the practical purpose of housing the women employees or the security men who, for one reason or another, weren't busy but had to remain on the grounds overnight. They had not been spared death.

It was nearly an hour before Costaign and Whitney had an accurate count of bodies.

"I make it twenty-nine," said the sheriff.

Both men returned to the porch of the hacienda. Whitney knew he should be making radio calls to half a dozen agencies instead of sitting there numbly lighting a cigarette, but he and Costaign both were so caught up in the fantasy of death and agony that they felt like observers at a shadow play.

"I never seen anything like it," the sheriff said. "Everybody dead. Everything."

"Incredible," Costaign answered.

"I been a cop for twenty-three years and I've never seen anything like this."

Deep in a shock like combat fatigue, they were as yet unable to absorb what they had seen, let alone, analyze it.

"Were you in the war, Sheriff?"

"Korea," the big man answered dully.

"I was never in the service. I guess this is what war is like."

"Yeah. A little bit. In a way this is worse. When you go into combat you're psyched up for it. You expect things. All the noise and the shit flying around. You expect to find dead people. You never like it. You're peeing your pants scared all the time, but you're expecting it. Here, it's more of a shock. You come to a place like this on a nice normal day in your normal life, you don't expect to find—all this. Same reason I never got used to automobile accidents. It always seemed kind of weird having a guy die outside the window of a Howard Johnson's."

Costaign nodded.

"Even in police work this is the worst. Worse than Juan Corona. Worse than the Trash Bag killings. Tell you the God's truth, Doc. I don't even know where to begin. This should have happened to a bigger man than me. I ain't the guy to handle the biggest murder that ever happened."

The very act of having to verbalize his thoughts seemed a spur to activity.

"Well, we got to start somewhere, and right now. I'll radio the station. Have them get in touch with the medical examiner. Get him and the crime lab people out here. Got to get this place sealed off. Oh, Christ, what a job of identification we're going to have. Doc, what do you think killed them all?"

"Well, I couldn't say without conducting some examinations. And I'd need the proper facilities," said Costaign.

"Give me a guess then. You seen a lot of things. Give me something to tell them when I get them on the horn."

"I don't know what to tell you. Not too much makes sense."

"Well, were they killed or weren't they? Murdered, I mean," the sheriff asked.

"Maybe they were. Maybe they weren't. Your medical examiner will have to tell you. I can't without an examination. Maybe they were poisoned."

"Sorry I snapped at you," the sheriff said, touching the doctor's arm. "I guess this thing has got to me. What about the wounds? What made these people look like they were skinned alive?"

"That's one of the things that doesn't make sense. You're right. They look as though their skin has been peeled, but the truth is the wounds are not that serious. Abrasions, mostly. I could see them causing a little psychological, maybe even a little physical, trauma, but I can't see them causing death. These kind of wounds wouldn't have affected the skin's breathing. You know, as it does when someone suffers extensive body burns. Burns cause different reactions."

"You mean they're the same kinds of wounds like you found on that girl this morning?"

"Just about," said Costaign.

"And you don't know what might have caused them?"

"Except for what we talked about in relation to her—the sadists—I have no idea. I don't imagine that theory holds up about twenty-nine people, does it?"

"You know, Doc, I don't believe a word you're telling me. No offense to you, but you got a look on your face like a dog caught eating shit. Maybe you don't know nothing, but you're sure as hell thinking something. Why don't you come right out and say it?"

Costaign looked at Whitney evenly. "Always the cop, huh? Nothing goes over your head. Okay. I've got some ideas. What they mean, I don't know. I *do* know I'm an M.D. and I am supposed to be an expert. I don't want to get quoted when I'm not sure."

"Go ahead. Shoot," said the sheriff.

"The only cause of death I can even imagine is an epidemic. It's the dead insects and animals. Okay, let's assume that there is somewhere on this earth a person so psychotic that he kills twenty-nine people—in some way we haven't figured out yet—and ends up scraping all their skin off. That's quite an assumption in itself. Can we imagine that same guy killing rabbits, prairie dogs, and about a million roaches?"

He looked around and went on. "No. It's got to be some kind of disease that kills any living thing it touches."

"What kind of disease could do *that* to a person?" the sheriff asked.

"Again I have to say I don't know. It would have to be something I've never heard about before. That doesn't make it impossible. Some diseases do strange things. The Bubonic Plague swells and discolors the face and the region around the groin. That's how it came to be known as the *Black* Plague. You know the poxes cause skin eruptions. Maybe this thing we're talking about causes such violent itching that the victim first tears off his clothes and then rolls around in sharp gravel. I've seen hives cause some pretty nasty reactions. I'd be willing to bet that some of these abrasions were caused by the person's own scratching fingernails."

"You're still making sense," said the sheriff. "How come that girl you found didn't die?"

"That's one of the great questions of medical science. How come two people are exposed to a disease and only one catches it? How come two people have the same disease, one dies and the other lives? Some people seem to survive everything—even inoperable cancer. Maybe the young woman had some kind of natural immunity."

"So what do we do?" the sheriff asked.

"Nothing. Once your coroner gets here it's his case."

The sheriff rose and ground his cigarette underfoot.

"The telephone inside is a lot closer than my car radio. I'll go make a couple of calls."

He returned a few minutes later and found Costaign still sitting in the same position.

"Wheels turning now?" Costaign asked.

"Well, yeah. Couple of little complications, but nothing serious. Ol' Doc Stryker at the coroner's office ain't available. He's in San Francisco, at a convention. In the meantime, they're going to get in touch with the state health department and have them send a doctor up here. I didn't want to tell them too much. I just said we had a serious problem that involved dead insects, so he's going to try to get this insect expert. Might take a little time for him to get here.

"Look, Doc, I don't want no panic until we find out what's going on. I'm asking you what you'd do if you were running the medical investigation. The office is going to call Doc Stryker back from San Francisco. I told them it was that important. What should we do till he gets here?"

Costaign reflected for a few seconds. "You did the right thing contacting the state health department. One of the first things we'd have to do under any circumstances would be to send some specimens to the

U.S. Health Department Communicable Disease Center in Atlanta.

"If it were my case, first thing I'd do is quarantine the entire area. So far the best theory we've got to explain the deaths is epidemic. If there is an epidemic, I wouldn't want a lot of strangers roaming around."

"That's done," said the sheriff. "I got roadblocks at both ends of the road leading up here, about a mile away in either direction. Got detour signs being set up in Cherakowa. Got the county highway department putting them up in other places."

"After that I guess I'd just sit on my tail until the fellow from the health department gets here. There isn't much else I could do. I think you did the right thing by keeping closed mouthed. I wouldn't do too much talking until we get our facts straight. You never can tell how the public will react."

The sheriff seemed to be considering Costaign's response. Then, as though something occurred to him for the first time, a series of expressions washed across his face.

Obviously having just made up his mind about something, the sheriff said, "I'm going into town. All the calling that I can do, I've done. Now I got some things I got to handle in person. I know it ain't fair for me to ask, but. . . ."

"You'd like me to stick around while you're gone," Costaign finished for him. Smiling.

"Well, yeah. I would. Kind of 'Hold the Fort,' you know. Maybe look around a little bit. Get the lay of the land. Why don't you move your car up from the parking lot. Put it in the inside garage here. It won't be in anybody's way once the investigation starts. What do you say?"

"Sure, Sheriff. I really don't mind at all. To tell you the truth, I like being up to my neck in the investigation. Besides that, if we have an epidemic here, I've been exposed to it. I shouldn't be wandering around either."

The sheriff shook the doctor's hand. "Thanks," he said.

"Want to walk to the lot with me?"

"No. Not just at the moment," said Costaign. "I'll get my car later. By the way, you're from around this part of the country, aren't you? What do you know about these outdoor cockroaches. I've been thinking a lot about them. Do you remember any instance of their transmitting an epidemic?"

"Only thing I know about roaches is that I hate the bastards. Kill them whenever I get the chance," Whitney answered.

"Okay. Hurry back, huh? I'm not sure how much I'm going to like hanging around this place alone."

The sheriff smiled, turned away, and marched across the compound as though he were on parade. Soon the sound of his car zooming away shattered the stillness.

The aura of death was thick in the air. No matter how hard he tried not to, Costaign found himself responding to his surroundings. Inanimate things: the hills, the sky, the air—all seemed suddenly hostile. Trees and rocks seemed to be cloaking horrors yet unknown.

He rose from the porch. This was as good a time as any to get the car.

He recalled his thoughts of the early morning, before he had found the woman, and it was easy for him to imagine now that some unknown agency had taken a hand in his affairs. He had wanted to know what it would be like to get away from the artificiality of the hotel and really grapple with life. Looking around, he wondered, What greater testing ground than this? Whether he liked it or not, he was involved. He'd told the sheriff the truth when he'd said he was glad. He had an eerie, sixth-sense feeling that before all this was over he would learn perhaps more about himself than he wanted to know.

His eyes fell on three corpses clustered around the Spanish fountain, and he conjured images of medieval Europe during The Plague. Was that what he was involved in? A new plague? Bodies by the thousands piled in the streets waiting to be carted away? What would this new plague be called? Perhaps The Red Plague. Would modern trucks rumble through the streets, their bullhorned drivers calling out, "Bring out your dead! Bring out your dead!"? Would Las Vegas be remembered as the place where it had begun? Would he be remembered as the first doctor who had come into contact with it?

On heavy legs he continued toward the parking lot. He seemed to be able to feel sickness moving around inside him. Once or twice he checked his skin. He had a feeling that he had passed through some sort of portal and the door had slammed behind him.

He tried not to listen to the wind; instead he listened for living sounds. A bird maybe, or a cricket. Some sign that life other than his own existed in this pocket of death. Nothing. Silence. He wondered if it were true that animals of the wild can sense danger, and immediately abandon the area.

He'd heard that at the moment of death, your whole life passes before you. He guessed that his noisome surroundings, plus the immediate danger of contracting a terminal disease, qualified as a first cousin to dying. Yet his thoughts were only scattered and disjointed.

Costaign wondered how he had been so calm about it with the sheriff on the porch. Perhaps because the sheriff had been another human being, and one human being can face even cosmic horror if he is accompanied by another human.

Suddenly he was terrified.

Minutes later, he pulled his VW into the house garage on the second level. Since the hacienda was built into a hill, the second story in the rear became the third story in the front, thanks to the downhill slope. The floor he parked on was also sloped toward the rear entrance door. Costaign pulled the car up to the kitchen entrance and cramped the wheels. Once inside the kitchen door, he passed another door to the right, the big metal entrance way to a walk-in refrigerator. That must make deliveries easier, he thought. He stood at the door and looked back at the car. Why should he bother to lock it? Who's going to steal it? he thought bitterly.

CHAPTER
THREE

"But an epidemic of what?"

"He says he don't know. Just that it could be," the sheriff replied. "Soon as I got to thinking about it, I figured I better talk to you."

Peter Lockwood, mayor of Cherakowa, rose from his desk and walked to the window. The section of his forehead between his eyes was clenched into a deep furrow. His grim expression seemed out of place in the bright knotty pine office, a room designed to promote self-confidence and a feeling of well-being.

On one wall a needlepoint said Smile. On the desk a shiny cardboard foldover advised Boost—Don't Knock. And on the back of the door, so it would be the last thing one saw as one left, a poster: *Have a Good Day.*

"He could be wrong," said Lockwood, as though he were pleading with the lawman for agreement.

"Well, sure he could. Like I say, he's only guessing. I figure, what the hell, he's a doctor. Maybe we ought to listen to him anyway."

"You see? You admit he could be wrong. I know these young doctors. They get one look and right away they think the worst. I think we have to get a handle on this situation. If we're not careful, it'll get blown all out of proportion and we'll have a panic situation on our hands. I see it as a matter of interpretation."

"Jesus Christ, Pete. A matter of interpretation? I got twenty-nine bodies up at Eros Ranch. How the hell am I supposed to interpret that?"

"Yes, I agree. It's a terrible thing that's happened."

The mayor paced the floor, tapping the fingers of his right hand into the palm of his left.

"And I certainly appreciate your position," he continued. "It's an awesome responsibility. I'm simply saying we have to keep our perspective."

He took up a position next to the sheriff and placed his hand on one massive shoulder.

"Tony, I'm glad you called me first. It shows me you've got all our best interests at heart. It shows me we've got the right man in office in Arapahoe County. After all, there are a lot of different angles to be considered, and we're all part of the team."

The mayor turned on his best public relations manner. "I don't have to tell you our big target right now is the Centennial Fiesta. We have to keep everything in its proper relation to that. Look at it this way, Tony: Some things can be changed and others can't, and we have to have the wisdom to know the difference. We have to make our moves so that they relate to the greatest good for the greatest amount of people.

"This fiesta is an iffy proposition. *If* everything goes the way we've planned it—*if*—then all of Cherakowa is in fat city. *If* one little thing goes wrong, it could put the kibosh on all of us. You know how skittish the public is. I don't have to tell you. So it's your job, yours and mine, and everyone else's involved, to see that nothing does go wrong.

"Now I'm not saying it's a small thing that happened up there in Eros—Dear Lord, it's terrible, and I know it—but those dead people—and look at it this way, Tony—those dead people are dead and nothing is going to bring them back. How we *handle* their deaths could make all the difference in the world to how this fiesta turns out. You see what I mean?"

The sheriff nodded.

"I've been giving it some quick thought. Let me bounce a couple of ideas off you," the mayor continued. "If we go along with this young doctor. What's his name?"

"Robert Costaign."

"Yes. Dr. Costaign. If we go along with him and alert the state health department about the possibility of an epidemic, in an hour it'll be on the radio; in six hours the TV; and it'll be in every paper in the country tomorrow. Twenty-nine deaths is big news. Look what Legionnaire's Disease did for that hotel in Philadelphia.

Why, by God, that hotel went right down the tube.

"We're small peanuts compared to that hotel. If it could do that to a big hotel, imagine what it could do to us. You know we've spent a fortune advertising this fiesta in Los Angeles and San Francisco, because that's where we're going to be getting our tourist customers from. Can you imagine what'll happen if the word gets out that there might be a serious epidemic in Cherakowa! It won't matter whether the epidemic is real or suspected. Tourists won't come within a hundred miles of here!

"We can't stall, Tony. That fair is this Sunday, and it runs for a week. If we don't make it then, we don't make it. It's now or never!"

Sheriff Whitney considered for a moment before he spoke.

"Well, sure. I understand. I kind of got my own fish frying, too. I got two years' savings wrapped up in that shooting gallery. But how can we change the fact that twenty-nine people are dead? And suppose it is an epidemic? It could kill every person in this fucking town."

"Look, Tony. I'm not a fellow who hides from facts. I'm saying, suppose we make those facts work for us instead of against us? We know talk of an epidemic will drive people away. Let's use the deaths to attract people. How? Mass murder! People are ghouls. After all the traffic accidents you've seen, you know that better than I do. They'll hang around in a thunderstorm just to see a drop of blood. And they'll travel twenty miles to see a place where a murder has been committed."

The mayor leaned across the desk and fixed the sheriff with his eyes. "What about these for headlines? TWENTY-NINE DEAD IN CHERAKOWA, NEVADA— GREATEST MASS MURDER IN HISTORY! Can you imagine the crowd that'll pull!"

Whitney looked at Lockwood as though the mayor had just shed his skin and become a lizard.

"Wait. Think about it. This county is your jurisdiction. You're the one who has the final say-so on what information is released. You don't have to let anyone go poking around if you don't want to."

"Oh, sure. I tell the local press that we got a mass murder. They tell the wire services. In ten minutes every newsman in the country knows about it. They all assign people to come out here with cameras. The networks. Everybody. Then I say, 'Sorry, boys, can't let you in.' That's just swell. While you're imagining things, imagine what that would do to us. By the time they finished speculating, it'd sound worse than an epidemic. I can see the headlines all right: IS ARAPAHOE COUNTY HIDING TWENTY-NINE ATOMIC DEATHS? And I'd be the worse sonofabitchin' sheriff since Bull Connor.

"Think about this, too. Everyone of them dead people has relatives, someplace. How long before they start howling around our ears? Suppose just one of them dead people comes from out of state. His relatives'll have the feds down on us· in a hot minute."

The mayor opened his mouth but said nothing.

"Be realistic, Pete. What makes you think tourists

are going to want to see a mass murder site where the murderer still hasn't been caught yet? They'll think: Christ, he might get me next.

"Then there's the big thing. If the doc is right and there really is an epidemic up there, the people in this town have a right to know about it. We could all be dead. How you going to have a fiesta when you're dead?"

The sheriff sat back as though his monologue had drained him. Lockwood's eyes became slits.

"You're right, Tony. About the mass murder and the press. It was just an idea off the top of my head. It gets back to the epidemic idea, doesn't it? And the way I see it, there's only one way for us," Lockwood said. His tone was significant.

"You asking me to hush this up?" said the sheriff.

"No, of course not." Lockwood paused as though his mouth were considering each word carefully, tasting it. "I am asking you," he said slowly, "just how necessary it is for the word to be spread immediately. Can't we keep it quiet a while?"

"For how long?"

"Just a few days," Lockwood answered. "Just so it doesn't throw a crimp into the fiesta. Let's give it a chance. It's important to all of us."

The sheriff was silent. Inside, he was being pulled in different directions.

"You know, Tony," the mayor continued, with ice chip eyes, "you're a pretty important man in this county. A lot of people look to you for guidance because they know you're not the sort of guy who goes off half-cocked. No, sir. You're the kind of man who thinks things through before he makes a decision. A lot of us think that a fellow with your talent won't be only a sheriff for very long. A fellow with your characteristics goes right to the top.

"I'm not suggesting that you do anything that goes against your conscience. Your code of honor and your sense of commitment are the things that would make a lot of us want to help you get to the top. Dammit, Tony, what I'm saying is, Why should we have a lot of damaging publicity right at the moment, when we're not even sure what's going on? What good can it do to start a lot of scare rumors? As I say, you're a fellow who never makes a decision without thinking it through."

There it was.

"Well," said Whitney, "we already got some things that's going to be hard to shut up. For one thing, we already got the doc up there. For another, I've already had my office talk to the state health department. Didn't tell nobody nothing, just that I needed a pathologist. They got some guy on the way. For all I know, he might be there right now."

"That does create a problem."

"What about the owners?" the sheriff went on. "How do I handle them? What about relatives?"

"Tony," Lockwood said evenly, "you do whatever you think is right and I'll back you. You can be the team captain on this one. Just as long as we all have our priorities in order."

Whitney fought to repress his anger, and his sense of *déjà vu*. It was Padney Flaherty's voice he was hearing all over again.

"You're right," he said, at last. "Okay. I'll be team captain."

He stood. He walked to the door. He felt he couldn't look at Pete Lockwood anymore.

"Remember, do what you have to do," Lockwood said to the big man's back, "but don't rush to do it."

Whitney slammed the door behind him. Have a good day!

Outside, in the parking lot, the late morning sun had contracted most of the shadows. God almighty! the sheriff thought. I've got to think this over. And quick.

Getting into his car, he sat for a long moment before he turned his key. He could hear the voice of Pete Lockwood swirling around in his head superimposed on the voice of Padney Flaherty. Was it Chicago all over again? Sure, do what you have to do and we'll back you—until you make a wrong move! Why the hell was it, all a guy wanted to do was to be a good cop, but so many other things seemed to get involved? Was he once again risking everything he had worked for?

He gunned the car and slid out into traffic. About a hundred yards down the street a red Pacer passed him, going in the opposite direction. Behind the wheel, a lovely dark-haired woman, twenty-six or twenty-seven, observed the banners and streamers through a pair of fashionably oversized glasses. The car had state license plates. On the center of both front doors was emblazoned the logo of the health department.

CHAPTER
FOUR

"I'm Dr. Symington," the young woman said, extending her hand, but not smiling. "You must be Dr. Costaign. The sheriff's office told me to expect you. I'm from the state health department."

"Hi." Costaign grinned.

He had been poking around the parked cars in the customers' lot trying to assemble what identification he could find for the sheriff, when her car turned into the access road.

"You don't know how glad I am to see you," he said.

Again she did not respond with a smile.

"I'm glad to see another human," Costaign said, as though he were explaining himself.

"If you'll show me where the body is, I think we can get started," she said.

She was dressed in a beige linen pants suit; a white blouse with an attached scarf that tied at the collar like a cravat. She was tall. Her lines were straight but not bony. Her hair hung slightly longer than shoulder length. Her face was a somewhat angular frame around brown eyes that didn't seem set deeply enough. They were wide and luminous behind her glasses.

Costaign flushed angrily at her peremptory manner. He'd seen it before, this defensive posture among women who were trying to make it in a world that heretofore had been the exclusive bailiwick of men. He felt it inappropriate at the moment. Remembering that she still hadn't seen the other side of the eucalyptus grove, he swallowed his anger.

"Okay. Let's go," he said.

She took up the brisk pace beside him as they headed for the grove.

"Dr. Kilrain, my department head, told me I'd be filling in for the medical examiner. My background is pathology," she stated.

"You didn't talk to the sheriff yourself?" Costaign asked.

"Yes. After Dr. Kilrain had given me the job."

"How much did the sheriff explain to you?"

"Not much," she answered. "He sounded upset. He just said he had a problem that needed a person with extensive entomology background."

Costaign stopped and looked directly at the young woman.

"If he didn't explain to you or Dr. Kilrain what's happened up here, maybe there are a couple of things you ought to know before we . . ."

"It might be easier if you explained it to me when we get where we're going," she said.

This time Costaign had to clamp down on his anger. Her manner clearly said that the amateurs were relieved, the professionals were here now.

"Of course," said Costaign. "I wouldn't want to hold up your schedule, but I think you may find a little more than you bargained for."

Screw her, he thought.

Side by side they strode into the grove. Her belled pants legs flapped at her ankles. She carried her medical bag in her right hand.

Just before breaking clear of the grove, the woman slowed her pace perceptibly, as though the same sixth sense that had tickled Costaign and Whitney earlier was now vibrating in her brain. She tilted her head as though she were listening. Her body became tense, her tread softer and more catlike. She even turned her face to Costaign, questioningly, but she did not know what question to ask.

Once out on the lawn, she stopped dead.

Again she looked at Costaign. This time the questions inside her seemed rammed against the inside of her teeth.

Remembering how he had felt the first time, he received no satisfaction from her crumbling imperiousness. Though her eyes had told him when he had met her that she had seen death, what could prepare a human for this?

He wanted to touch her, then decided it wouldn't be a

proper gesture. He had to hand it to her: She was holding up.

She allowed herself to be led to the porch, where she sat next to Costaign smoking a cigarette, collecting herself. Her eyes were fixed on the carpet of roaches, through which they had just crunched, and the three still-uncovered bodies near the fountain. He knew what she was feeling. There was more here than the visible signs of death. There was a *geist*, an atmosphere, a sucking-drain quality in the air. They sat in silence because talk was impossible at this moment.

Suddenly she stood, threw her half-finished cigarette on the stair, and stepped on it.

"I'm sorry. I guess I got carried away," she said. "It was very unprofessional."

"You've got nothing to be ashamed of. You should have seen the sheriff and me this morning."

For the first time, she smiled. It was a faint smile, but there was strength in her voice, the arrogance gone.

"Guess we might as well get to work right here," she said.

Between them, they worked out a procedure. He would help her move one of the bodies into the house, to the steel table he had noticed in the kitchen. She would be able to conduct some of the salient examinations, while he collected some of the dead insects and animals and prepared them for shipment to the health department lab in Atlanta.

Once the kitchen was set up as her impromptu work area, he knew there was little else he could do to help her. He felt better knowing that the investigation was in progress. He was also impressed at the control she exerted on herself. He wondered that the aura inside the house—the terror-filled expression of the corpses, the silence, the dark corners, the creaking of the house's warming joints—did not have greater effect on her.

"I'll be right outside if you need me for anything," he said.

"What could I need?" It wasn't a challenge. It was a question. He'd been there longer. Perhaps he knew something.

"I don't know. Anything."

Patricia Symington, M.D., went quickly and skillfully to work. She evaluated the exterior appearance of the body before her, then jotted down some notes for herself. She made examinations of the eyes, the ears. She smelled the breath, or rather she smelled the mouth whose breath was now part of the universe. So far the work was automatic.

Automatic work was like a mantra to her, occupying her conscious mind while her subconscious became free to wander. She thought about herself. She compared what she was doing at the moment to what it meant to be *Dr.* Patricia Symington.

She had known, of course, when she had become a doctor that she would be dealing with human illness, but she'd somehow seen it as the rather angelic work of relieving pain. She always visualized the happy, grateful expressions of her patients *after* the treatment was over; she had never thought of the treatment itself:

the stench of corrupted flesh; the pain; the snap but correct decisions that would have to be made. Though she knew this, it was not how she saw herself as a doctor, not entirely. She would be dishonest if she didn't admit that she had also seen the status. To be a doctor was to be honored. To be somebody. To make money. In a strange way, she had somehow seen her position and status as a vehicle for removing her from run-of-the-mill people. An aristocrat among aristocrats. And yet . . .

Costaign stood on the porch while the early afternoon sun turned white. One-thirty. How long would it take the crime lab people to get here? Should they even be allowed in until Dr. Symington found out what sort of disease they were dealing with?

He thought about the woman alone in the dreadsome ambiance of the house. He wondered what her first name was. Maybe she didn't have one. Maybe she had been born *Doctor* Symington. He wondered, too, about this feeling of foreboding. Usually such things pass when the worst has been faced, and surely these twenty-nine dead bodies were the worst. Yet his sixth sense told him that there was more horror to come.

Banzo was locked up in a cell by himself. What a cheese-eating, fuckin' place, he thought as he confronted the bars that looked through a weird glass window out onto the side of a hill. He lifted his hands and grasped the bars. He noted the cross tattooed between the thumb and first finger of his right hand. In the same spot on his left hand, the tattooed word *Hate*.

"Dangerous" that hillbilly sheriff had called him. Shit, that was one of the nicest things he'd been called in his life. He looked at the word *Hate* and said to himself, *right on*.

Why the fuck shouldn't he hate? What had the world ever shown him? People were liars and double-crossers, every single time; even chicks were full of shit. Everybody got you to do their dirty work and then when it was finished, man, all they wanted to do was sweep you under the carpet. The only place you met real people was in your gang. Nobody mattered but them. They looked after you and you looked after them. Who needed the rest of these maggots?

Banzo walked to the barred wall that constituted the doorway to his cell. He ran his hands along the bars like a kid dragging a stick along a picket fence. He noted the tan corridor outside the door, the heavy redolence of disinfectant, the diffused lighting from inset overhead bulbs. It was nothing new to him.

Back on his bunk again, he had nothing to do but think. And he hated these moments. When his mind turned inward on itself, there was no clear progression of thoughts; he saw instead a swirl of pictures, grotesque most of the time, distorted, and always seeming to center around a—figure. The figure he could never clearly see, but it was always there. A shrink had told him about it once. A lot of big, phony words. A motivation, or something like that, repressed.

As he had always done, Banzo forced a series of other

pictures between himself and the figure. He saw the gang, the one thing he drew satisfaction from. He saw them all back in Oakland, California, along San Pablo Avenue, hanging out in the Silver Eagle. He could almost taste the beer and hear the jukebox playing.

They were the baddest all right: him and the gang. Each had a Harley, and, man, that ain't no easy thing, for a whole gang to have Harleys. They were hard to find. When they went riding nobody fucked with them. One smartass did one day, waiting for a light. Man, Banzo had whacked an iron bar right through his windshield. In the Eagle, nobody got heavy either. They had one end of the bar that was all theirs, and nobody came down to it less they were asked. That meant mamas. Carlos, the owner—it didn't seem like he was afraid of them, though. He liked to have them around. The *Slavers* they were called. They had black and blue colors. Dig it?

There were six others in the gang besides himself: Cutter, Boris, Carmine, Ritter, Bird, Patton. Nice guys, but not a fucking brain among them. Tough as six-day old steak, but without him to tell them what to do they'd be just a bunch of hoods hanging out.

In the distance, down the corridor, Banzo heard a door slam. Must be somebody coming in or out. It didn't slide like a cell door would have. With the sound, his images of the gang and Oakland and beer and mamas shattered, and again he was confronted with the hidden image. For one wild moment, he thought the image had leaped from his mind out into the hall, until he realized that the uniformed figure in front of him was real. It was the hick sheriff, standing there in his uniform, with his gun hanging heavily on his hip.

It was almost a moment of recognition for Banzo. The man seemed to be the personification of his inner core of hatred. For one instant Banzo could almost see clearly into himself.

"What the hell are you dreaming about? The birdies in May?" Whitney asked.

Costaign began collecting specimens. He carried a canvas handbag some poor woman had left in the house, and a handful of medical specimen bags Dr. Symington had given him. He picked up a dead rabbit first. As he worked his way across the lawn toward the mobile home area, he picked up several handfuls of dead roaches, a dead locust, a cricket, a prairie dog, and a sparrow.

Soon he was beyond the farthest mobile home, flat against the sheer gulley wall. On impulse, he started to climb, leaving the bags behind. He told himself that he wanted an overall view of the ranch. Planting his feet, duck fashion, and clawing with his hands, he worked his way to the crest, kicking small avalanches behind him.

He dragged himself over the top and lay puffing. Whew! I'm in great shape for a guy who's not going to be thirty until this December!

He found himself on a wide shelf of land that seemed to move off several hundred yards before it joined the foothills of a steeper, rockier mountainside. Looking down at the ranch, Costaign smiled to himself. A real western phenomenon, he thought, like Grand Canyon. When you are in the bottom, down where the hacienda is located, you seem to be surrounded by Himalayan-like mountains; once you get to the top, though, you realize you have been at the bottom of a big hole.

Costaign studied the r nch. Even from there, it did not lose its aura off ominousness. Something else: From here he could see that the ranch didn't lay in a cul-de-sac, as he had originally thought. The gulley was really the great widening of an arroyo that ran down from the top of the mountain. Probably from Lake Campbell. He wondered how the ranch owners handled the possibility of flash floods, always a threat in this part of the world, especially when you're sitting in the middle of a waterway.

He turned his attention to the other direction, to the high cyclone wire fence that ran the length of the gulley lip, about a hundred yards in closer toward him. Probably part of the security setup. He wondered if it were electrified. Deciding to check it out, he rose to his feet and took about five steps, when suddenly the ground gave out from under him!

"Hey!" he shouted instinctively.

He was sunk up to his knees in dry, sandy soil that drifted downward around him like sand through an hourglass! He tried to move, and his footing collapsed even further. He sunk completely up to mid-thigh! He felt caught in some sort of arid quicksand. The circle of disappearing earth around him moved slowly away. The more he tried to escape, the deeper he sank, the more ineluctably the circle moved out! He was gripped by a flush of hot panic.

The earth shifted beneath him once more and he sank deeper! The indentation he now stood in was a good six feet across. His panic turned to bellowing terror as he realized he had disturbed a giant nest of cockroaches!! Hundreds of them swarmed out of the ground and scuttled over him!

Some survival instinct told him what to do. He threw himself, for all his repulsion, flat down onto the sinking earth, into the gathering carpet of roaches! He clawed his way like a swimmer, thereby distributing his weight more evenly. The cockroaches, with their swift, stiff-legged scuttle, swarmed his arms and back. He screamed again as he felt them tickle their way across his face! He ripped at the earth like a madman until, at last, he felt solid ground under him again.

Regaining his feet, he danced madly as he slapped and battered the hideous creatures from his clothes.

"What happened?" Pat Symington asked as Costaign walked into the kitchen.

"I decided to do a little exploring and I walked over a goddam spot the prairie dogs had undermined. The whole thing caved in underneath me."

"You look like a little kid, all covered with dirt like that." Pat smiled.

"That's not the worst of it. Some roaches must have

been nesting in this network of tunnels. When I went through, I disturbed them. Christ! What a feeling. They started crawling all over me."

"Doctor," she said, "why don't you go into the bar and make yourself a drink. It would be good therapy for you. I'm just about finished up out here. You could make one for me, if you'd like. I'll meet you in the bar in a minute. We've got some things to talk about."

"My first name is Roberto. Why don't you call me Bob? We're not exactly on staff floor together."

"All right, Bob. But you still look like a little kid."

"Okay, mama. I'll wash up, too," he said. "What's your name? It doesn't say doctor on your birth certificate, does it?"

"Except for the attending physician, no. Patricia. Pat, if you like."

"Great," Costaign said as he turned away. "See you in a couple of minutes."

After she'd taken care of the last details, Pat met him in the parlor.

"Let's go out on the porch," he suggested. "Frankly, this place gives me the creeps."

They sat again at the head of the stairs. He had brought her drink along. "Like Scotch on the rocks?"

"I could use about anything now," she answered.

"I haven't been able to confirm your epidemic theory. Nothing isolates out. No microbes, anyhow, that I can pick up with the equipment I have. Not on the humans or on the roaches. Maybe the electronic mics at our place or in Atlanta will come up with a virus."

"Not even an infiltration?" he asked.

"Nothing."

"Funny," said Costaign.

"You and Sheriff Whitney may have been too busy this morning to notice, but all the roaches died of having been physically crushed in one form or another. Not disease."

"*All* these roaches have been crushed? I don't believe it. How?"

"Taking your questions in the order of their appearance, yes, all the ones I examined; I'm sorry; and I haven't the vaguest idea."

"What about the humans? If they didn't die of disease, what did they die from?"

Pat looked at Costaign evenly. "Traumatic asphyxia."

"What?"

"That's right. The man on the examination table and two or three others I looked at while you were out were all strangled."

"But ..."

"Their throats were stuffed with cockroaches."

CHAPTER
FIVE

Before either could pursue the thought further, they were distracted by the hum of an automobile engine in the distance, apparently approaching up the access road. Both doctors smiled, making no effort to hide their relief.

"That must be the crime lab people," Costaign said.

"And about time, too. It's two-fifteen. I can't imagine what the sheriff had to do in town that would take this long for him to have sent the investigators."

They hurried down the stairs, out onto the lawn, as the hum became an increasing roar. In a moment, they were confronted by a sight that suggested anything but a coroner's investigating team.

Bouncing, rollicking, and slaloming among the eucalyptus trees, creating behind it a cloud of dust, roared a vintage white Cadillac convertible that was covered with dirt and looked as though it had been the losing entry in a demolition derby. The engine howled. The springs moaned. The protracted trumpeting of the horn ricocheted around the canyon.

Piled into the car were five outrageously happy young people, two men and three women. The men hooted, the women squealed. The women's hair snapped out behind them like banners. Wherever they had been, they'd had one hell of a time.

The doctors stared uncomprehendingly.

The car, weaving and jerking, plowed its way up to the Spanish fountain, then braked so hard its rear end fishtailed. There was a moment of stillness, during which Pat clutched Bob's arm, then a diastolic chorus of human shrieks. The driver gunned the engine and the car lunged backward.

"Hey! Wait a minute!' Costaign shouted as he and Pat started for the car. Before they had taken five steps, the car lurched into a semicircle, then, in another cloud of dust, raced for the main entrance. The women's screams continued. A male voice said, "Jesus Christ almighty!"

"Don't bother," said Costaign, gripping Pat's arm, "they're running like scared rabbits. We'll never catch them. Let them go. Goddamit, I thought Whitney had this area sealed off."

"I hope they go straight to the police. It's better than their getting hysterical all over town."

They walked disconsolately back to the porch.

"It's a tough break for them to stumble on a scene like this without any warning," Costaign said as they sat.

"I hope they don't panic the town."

"We didn't have a chance to discuss it before that car showed up, but when the sheriff gets back he's going to want some answers," Costaign said.

"I've given you all the answers I've got. Every person died of traumatic asphyxia. I have no doubt you'll find some died of heart attacks brought on by the strangulation, but the cause of death was strangulation."

"The sheriff's theory was that this is a mass murder. What kind of maniac—or maniacs—goes around strangling twenty-nine people by stuffing their throats with cockroaches?"

The woman shook her head. "No mass murder, either," she said.

"Then what the hell is it?"

"It's got to be disease of some incredibly bizarre type. As bizarre as it may turn out to be, it's the only thing that makes any sense."

"That's the way I feel. I've even thought about the possibility of some form of radiation poisoning, but I can't get that to work out either. I thought about fear-induced heart failure, judging from the looks on the faces, and that doesn't come up right. All I'm sure of is that nobody goes around stuffing twenty-nine throats full of roaches."

"Not only throats," Pat said, looking at him, "every natural orifice is stuffed: throats, mouths, ears, eyes, anuses, and vulvae."

Costaign looked at her as though she had hit him. But before he could say anything the conversation was cut short by the reappearance of the Cadillac convertible. Again the two doctors stood to meet it.

There was no joy in the vehicle this time. Grimly, tentatively, it worked its way across the grounds, stopping about twenty feet from them. The two doctors walked toward it. Soft sobbing could be heard as the five people slowly emerged.

One of the two men, a bruiser who reminded Costaign of Sheriff Whitney, was pressing a bloody handkerchief to his left eye.

"I'm surprised you're back," Costaign said to the newcomers. "I thought you'd be at the sheriff's office by this time." To the big man: "You all right?"

"Yeah," he growled.

The other passengers formed a knot around him. All of them looking stunned.

"Maybe you'd better let me have a look at it. I'm a doctor. That eye might be hurt worse than you think," said Costaign.

"Later," said the big man. "Not now. I'm still boiling. What the hell happened here?"

"Bullshit," said Pat, marching up to the injured man, catching him off guard with her unexpected use of profanity. Looking at the five numb faces, she knew someone had to take charge. "I'm a doctor, too, and you're going to sit right over here on the porch while I have a look at that eye. It's bad enough you drive like a maniac, you needn't talk like one."

The big man allowed himself to be led to the porch.

"You," Pat said to one of the women, a blonde, bare-legged in a pink, mid-calf dress, teary eyed, and looking one minute away from hysteria, "on the back of the front door over there, just inside, you'll find a black medical bag. Would you get it for me, please?"

The woman, too, moved without question.

"Now, you," she said to her patient, "take the handkerchief away. How'd you hurt yourself, hotshot? Bouncing off the dashboard?"

The injured man glowered at her.

"No," said the other man, who also seemed angry enough to erupt like a volcano, "he got it from one of your frigging deputies down at the roadblock. If those maggots hadn't pulled their guns, that bastard with the stick'd have his head smeared all over that road."

The man who had just spoken was as tall as a coconut palm, and just as thin and rangy. His hair hung shaggily around his head like fronds. His blue eyes looked out over craggy features. His teeth were as even as piano keys. His long arms hung to his sides. His fists were balled. He wore a blue leisure suit that looked as though it had not been off him in days. Beneath the jacket, he wore a pale blue sports shirt. A gold coke spoon dangled on a thin gold chain against the hair of his chest.

"And that sumbitch ain't off the hook yet," he said, looking at his injured friend.

After thanking the blonde for her bag, Pat said, "I'm Dr. Patricia Symington. This is Dr. Roberto Costaign. Who are you?"

The injured man paid no attention to the question.

The tall man looked at the two doctors. "You cops?"

"I told you, we're doctors," said Pat.

"Cops got doctors."

"I'm with the state health department. Dr. Costaign is in private practice."

"I'm house physician at the Sunburst Hotel on the Vegas Strip. The sheriff and I were the first to discover the bodies. We're holding down the fort until the coroner's people get here."

"I'm Long John Markley," said the tall man. "That's Big Jim Goodman. We been working a construction job in Vegas. Just got paid off. We're doing a little celebrating. This lady," he put his arm around the woman who had fetched the medical bag, "is Candy Ackerman. She's from Oklahoma City."

"I'm Irene Ludlow," said the tall redhead dressed in blouse and pants. She stood behind Long John, cradling the blond head of the third woman. "This is Katie Murtagh."

"Oh my God!" Katie suddenly screamed, dislodging herself from Irene. "How can you talk about names? With this!" She swung her arm around to indicate the house and grounds, then again dissolved into tears as Irene pulled her close.

"You say the sheriff's men at the roadblock did this to you?" Pat asked.

"Yeah," Big Jim grunted.

"What for?"

"How the hell would I know?"

"Them bastards at the roadblock, all right," said Long John. "All we did was try to get through, and they tell us we got to get back here. We tell them, 'Hey, man, there's a disaster up there.' They say they don't care, we gotta come up here right now. We say, 'Shit, we'll be glad to lend a hand if you need help, but first let us take the chicks into town.' They say, 'What do you want to do, spread germs around?' Next thing you know, we're having a couple of words, and without a peep, man, this cop lets the big guy over there have it across the skull. Then they all whip out their artillery. Shit, it looked like old Dodge City: all these dudes with guns. They say, 'Don't bother trying to get out the other way, we got guys up there, too.' So we come back. They wasn't screwing with them guns, I'll tell you. That's okay. We know a way."

"You mean they wouldn't let you out?" asked Costaign.

"That's what I'm saying, Doc."

"How'd you get in past them?" Pat asked.

"We didn't exactly come right from the outside last time you seen us. We picked the girls up here at the house yesterday after we finished work and got paid off. We got a lot of food and juice and spent the night in a little cabin. Up there." He pointed to a wooded area of the hill behind the hacienda. "There's a little place where you can have a private party. Which is what we were doing, having a private party."

"Can you drive to this place?" Costaign asked.

"Not all the way. There's a private road down by the parking lot that leads up, but you can only drive about a hundred feet, then you gotta walk."

Katie shrieked again. "You're all crazy! You're all

crazy! Talk! Cars! Roads! Oh my God! What happened to everybody? Everybody's dead!"

"Let it out, babe," Irene said as she cradled the woman. Candy was quickly infected by the panic. Long John held her tight as she sobbed in hopeless agony.

"The girl's got a good question, Doc. What did happen?" Long John asked. "These three work here. The dead people, the other girls, are their friends."

"I'm sorry," said Costaign and went on to explain as much as he knew. As he talked the two hysterical women quieted down into something like shock.

Pat, having finished with Big Jim, observed the expressions on Candy and Katie and knew it was time for her to jump in again.

"We can talk about all this later," she said. "Right now we have a lot of work to do. We don't know what time the sheriff'll be back. We can use all the help we can get."

"What do you want us to do?" Big Jim asked, standing, rubbing the newly applied bandage. "Thanks for the patch." He knew what she was trying to accomplish.

"First of all, I think we'd better do something about the—bodies. It's getting late. They've been lying out all day. Would you fellows help move them into the house? There's a medical closet near the main stairway, you'll find a litter there."

The two men headed inside. "You, too, will you, Bob?" she said to Costaign. He nodded and joined the other two.

She turned to the women. "Would you guys help me

clean up inside? When the coroner gets here, he's going to need a clean area in which to work."

Pat immediately recognized Irene as the strength among the women and felt a bond with her. It didn't matter that it was an ambivalent bond of attraction-repulsion. After Pat had put Candy and Katie to work cleaning up the parlor floor, she pulled Irene aside.

"Do you—work here?" Pat asked.

The redhead nodded, not defiantly, but firmly, as though she expected the same shocked response she usually got from women when they discovered she worked in a brothel.

Pat's face remained unmoved. Irene liked that.

"Then you'd know the other women?" Pat asked.

"I'd know them."

"Do you feel up to doing a dirty job? I know it's an awful thing I'm asking, but you seem more pulled together than Candy and Katie. I need someone to make identifications. It won't be easy. . . ."

"Sure. I'll do it," Irene said laconically.

"You don't have to."

"I'll do it. What the hell. If they can die, I guess I can look at them."

"Thanks." Pat squeezed Irene's arm. "I'll get you a notepad and a ballpoint. You can stand inside the garage door when the men bring in the bodies."

Returning to the parlor, Pat found Katie sitting disconsolately on one of the circular divans. Candy was missing.

"She went to make a phone call," Katie said, looking up.

Pat almost ran to retrieve Candy, when it occurred to her that the sheriff, in the interest of secrecy, had probably had all the phone calls rerouted to his office. Or had had service cut off. She turned again to Katie.

"You were in a cabin up behind the house all last night?"

"Uh-huh," Katie nodded.

"Didn't you hear any noises? Any sounds at all?"

"Why did it have to happen?" said Katie, shaking her head. "They were all good kids. They never hurt nobody. Why would God let this happen?"

"Come on," said Pat gently, "let's get started on the floor."

Costaign and Pat had decided to store the bodies in the large walk-in kitchen refrigerator. Outside the garage entrance leading to the kitchen, Irene leaned against the wall with a pen and notebook in hand. From out of the afternoon slices of dark shadow thrown down from the ridge, the grim parade proceeded. One by one the victims were carried by. The three men would bring the litter to a stop for a moment, a hand would pull back the sheet, Irene would stare into the hideously skinless, crimson mask, looking for familiar features. God, how death twisted a human face. Irene would either nod or shake her head, while her own face was clamped tightly as an iron door. Another hand would return the sheet, and the men would continue on. As they did they would leave her alone with the shafts of sunlight that pierced the trees and left leprous handprints on the ground. Neither Bosch nor Doré could have created scenes of such eerie silence, distorted color, and horror.

Life by life, the awesome procession passed Irene. Sometimes, she would make no notation. Sometimes as the men crunched away, she'd write, *No. 9: Judy Wallace, 23, divorced, lived in Vegas, one child, from Los Angeles.* Each time, the men would look at Irene and become just a little frightened that such courage exists.

The last body they carried in was the remains of a plump, large-bosomed brunette. Irene had prayed all afternoon that this body would not pass her. With the failure of her prayer, a little of her iron failed, too. She moved her head not at all, but her hands, both of them, dropped to her sides. Long John nodded significantly to the other men, and they moved on silently.

A minute later, Long John returned alone. Irene hadn't moved an inch.

"She was the last one. Come on inside and have a drink."

The woman nodded. The shadows of late afternoon had etched themselves into the hollows of her cheeks. Her eyes were empty.

"You knew her pretty well, didn't you?" he asked.

Again, Irene only nodded.

"You're one hell of a soldier, Renie," Long John said softly. "I don't know too many guys who could have done what you just did. And I've known the baddest."

"Now that they're all gone, it looks like nothing happened," she said.

Long John tried to imagine Irene's being anything different from what she was now. Had there been a last night? Had there been a this morning? Had there been booze and grass? Had Big Jim and Candy and Katie really ever laughingly pinned her to the bear rug in front of the cabin fireplace while he'd licked champagne from the hollows of her giggling body?

Long John stepped closer.

"Don't touch me, Johnny, okay? I'll be okay if you just don't touch me."

"Sure. Here." He handed her a lit cigarette.

"Thanks." She took a deep drag. Her exhalation was labored, as though she were trying to expel all the ghastliness she had absorbed.

"She was a long-time pal of yours, huh?"

"Yeah."

"I guess I know how you feel. I'd be pretty ripped up if anything happened to that big guy inside," he said.

"Why are they all dead, Johnny? What happened?"

"I don't know. I don't know nothing. The doc says some kind of disease. Shit. I don't know. Let's go inside."

"Do you think we'll die like that, too?" she asked.

"I don't think about it. Don't you neither. We got too many other things to worry about. Come on." He had to restrain himself from putting his arm around her.

As they walked, Irene said numbly, "Her name was Vivian. You almost asked her along with you last night. She was a good friend of Candy and Katie. But you like skinny ones. So you asked me instead."

Long John didn't answer.

Desert mountain air is thin and dry. It has no

substance in itself, it merely reflects: during the day, the candle flame heat of the sun; at night, the chill of the stars.

There is an hour or so around late afternoon when the sun becomes weak and the air cools immediately. The earth, the sand and rocks, which has absorbed heat all day, begins to return it to the air. The desert mountain becomes hot and cold at the same time. A man may walk along with warm feet and tingling cheeks.

During this period, nature gets restive. Prairie dogs pop their heads out of their burrows and look around. Desert birds swoop and soar. Scorpions scratch to the surface and prepare for their dances of love. The trees—in the mountains there are trees—shake their branches like skirts. What life there is, moves then.

No prairie dogs peeked at Eros Ranch, nor did the scorpions dance. Even the trees hung still. Which is not to say there was no life. *Something* lived. Something unseen that exuded menace. Something that had taken all the healthy life of the desert and had perverted it to its own blasphemous ends. Something that waited.

Together Irene and Long John stepped into the parlor. Someone had turned the lights on. The divans had been drawn into a loose circle. Their occupants seemed to be engaged in council.

"This is absurd," Pat was saying. "It's nearly five o'clock and nobody has shown up. We haven't heard from the sheriff. I can't even call my office. We have no idea what's going on. How long does the sheriff expect us to stay here without word? I think it's time we went into town and got this straightened out."

"The phone's out, too," Candy said.

"Good luck trying to get through that roadblock," said Big Jim.

Irene handed the notebook to Pat, then dropped heavily onto one of the divans. Long John went to the bar in the adjoining room. "Get you a pop?" he called over his shoulder.

"Thank you," said Irene.

"I don't think the phone's dead," said Costaign. "It's jacked into the sheriff's office. I'm not sure what we ought to do. The sheriff must have his reasons. There may be something going on that we don't know about. I think we ought to sit tight until some things get clarified."

"Stay here? How long? It's almost dark. I couldn't stay here in the dark," said Katie, her voice gradually rising.

"Katie, I can assure you we're all as eager to get out of this place as you are, but the sheriff has asked us to stick around until we establish whether we're dealing with a possible epidemic. Don't worry, the sheriff'll get us out of here just as soon as he can," said Costaign.

"You bet your ass he will," said Long John, returning from the bar, bringing a bottle of Jim Beam and several glasses containing ice cubes, and sitting next to Irene on the divan. "And he's got till I finish this drink to do it. Katie's right. I ain't hanging around this rat's nest after dark either. If that sheriff ain't here: tough noogies. Ain't no redneck sheriff going to make me stay where I don't want to be. Soon as I finish this drink, we're splitting, sheriff or no sheriff."

Big Jim gave an approving nod from the chair, and there was instant agreement among the women that they would join them.

Costaign felt himself in charge as long as the sheriff wasn't there. He was used to people's listening to him. He looked at Pat and felt that he had to somehow gain control of the situation or he would lose status in her eyes. He wondered why that was important to him.

"I think Dr. Costaign has a point," Pat said, before Costaign had a chance to answer. "After all, he's the one who recommended the sheriff isolate this area. It's a fact we may have a communicable disease here. We'd be a menace to ourselves and to everybody else if we were to leave now. The sheriff is doing what's right. I think we ought to give him the benefit of the doubt."

"Screw that," said Long John. "We know a way out around them roadblocks. Soon's this drink's finished, we're taking off and the girls are coming with us. You and the other doc here can come along if you want, or not. Whatever's right."

A silence settled over the group. The last word seemed to have been said on the subject. Costaign looked at Long John with anger that he had made him look bad in front of Pat. He had not merely challenged Costaign's "authority," he had swept it aside, making him look ineffectual. Yet, even in his anger, other thoughts plagued Costaign.

Why were Long John and Big Jim in such a hurry to leave? Did they, too, sense an impending disaster, worse than the one that had occurred? Was their sixth sense telling them something? Both Big Jim and Long John seemed old in experience. Candy had told Costaign earlier that they had done two tours in Viet Nam together: one in the Pacification Program, the other, training Cambodian Rangers. They must be finely tuned to such sensations.

By five-forty-five, the gulley of Eros Ranch was a solid shadow. The sun, having passed the peaks of the highest surrounding mountains, bounced its rays on to more distant places. So bright was the sky compared to the ground, you might think the rays were glad to avoid the accursed brothel.

The one drink had turned to two, then to three, stretching out the departure deadline. The group had broken up. Long John and Irene had gone to the bar. Bob and Pat had gone into the kitchen. At the front door, Candy and Katie stood behind Big Jim, as if for protection from the gathering darkness.

Katie said, "It's like I keep expecting to see all the people again, you know? I can almost feel them around. Like they'll all jump up and say the whole thing was a joke. I can't believe they're all dead. I still can't believe it. Oh, it's awful. I keep expecting to hear the stereo, and see all the girls, and see the johns coming in."

"Don't worry, baby," Big Jim said. "We'll be out of here pretty quick now."

Yet each suspected that his fate was somehow tied in

with the house. Big Jim's eyes scanned the outdoors in a practiced manner. First he put them out of focus, then let them slowly drift from the left side of his vision field to the right. This way, his eyes, which could not distinguish individual figures, could detect the slightest movement. It was a trick he'd learned in Nam. He scanned back and forth several times, with no result. What was he looking for? Maybe the place was getting to him. He wondered what his pal John was thinking. Did he have the same feelings? He could not shake the idea that *something* was out there.

It reminded him of the time he and the "long guy" had been on the fire-base alert line around Khe San, the night before the Tet offensive. They hadn't seen Viet Cong for weeks, except for an occasional round. Yet all of a sudden, that night, they knew.

"Now, Big Jim turned his head. "Hey! Long boy!" he shouted.

"What?"

"C'mere a minute."

Long John, accompanied by Irene, was soon standing next to him. The woman stepped back as though the men had business that didn't concern them.

"Look. Out there," said Big Jim.

"Look at what?"

"Just look."

Pat and Costaign walked in from the kitchen and also stood silently watching the two men.

"I don't see nothing," Long John said.

"Me neither," said Big Jim.

Long John turned his head toward his friend. The two men were close, had been through too much together, for Long John to miss his meaning.

"Anything?" Big Jim asked.

"Maybe." A beat. "Ain't going to find out till I take a smell."

"Right," said Big Jim. Turning to Katie, Candy, and Irene, he said, "Long John and me are going for the car. We'll drive it up to the porch. You girls can hop in and we'll take off." To Costaign and Symington: "You coming?"

"Look," Costaign began, "we have a potentially dangerous situation here. If there's an epidemic . . ."

"Oh, shit," said Big Jim.

Long John swung the front door open, and the two men stepped out onto the porch.

"Hey, wait! Don't leave. Let's see if we hear from the sheriff," Costaign called, hurrying after them. He dropped into silence when he realized he was talking to their backs.

Big Jim and Long John had traversed the lawn about halfway to the parked convertible, when suddenly the hillcrest above the mobile homes erupted with half a dozen muzzle blasts!

A storm of bullets spattered the earth between the two men and the car! Several slugs thunked into the porch!

In a chorus of shrieks, the women dived back in through the door. Costaign, flat on his face inside the door, shouted to the two men on the lawn.

As the first bullet struck the ground, they, with the

swiftness of a pair of mongooses, hurled themselves through the air. Hitting the ground, they rolled and, in a single continuous motion, regained their feet and ducked into the garage.

Costaign slammed the door!

CHAPTER SIX

Anton Whitney, sitting alone at a table in Harry Shapiro's Dew Drop Inn, slugged his bourbon on the rocks in a single gulp, then waved to Harry for a refill.

"Working up an appetite, Tony?" Shapiro asked, smiling broadly.

"Nope. Just drinking."

The sheriff did not return Harry's smile. His face remained a mask of vague concern. He looked at Harry as though he were searching for something in the man's face, and the steadiness of his gaze disconcerted the bar owner.

"I know how you feel," Harry said. "Must be the fiesta. Driving you nuts, huh? Me, too."

When the sheriff did not reply, Harry returned

awkwardly to the bar. "Just holler when you need a refill," he called over his shoulder.

The sheriff watched Harry engage two young carny workers in a conversation about stream fishing. Harry's voice seemed too loud, too strident.

There were three other lone drinkers at the bar. Around the room, several tables, maybe four or five, were filled with fiesta concession workers. Harry's doing all right, Whitney thought. More business than he's had at this hour for a long time. He looked long at Harry, wishing his eyes were an X-ray machine so that he could see what was inside.

There was more to him than the five feet seven, stocky frame. He'd always liked Harry. He'd always been good for a fishing trip, or a couple of laughs, and he sure wasn't slow at buying a drink. Was that all there was? What did he think? Was his whole life just a matter of buying and selling booze? Did he have any values beyond the jokes and the banal bar conversations? How about Chuck Caine who ran the drugstore? Or Will Apperson who ran the Howard Johnson's out on the highway? Sometimes they seemed like great guys, individuals with distinct characteristics, but sometimes they seemed to represent a type that Whitney was coming to fear and despise.

Businessmen. They were okay when you met them just as people, but when they took over their jobs they seemed to become something else. They did things that their "principles of sound business" made them do. Whether they liked what they had to do or not, they still did it. Even more important, they seemed to have all the power.

In retrospect, Whitney could trace all the troubles he'd ever had to them. He'd been a good cop in Chicago until he'd gotten mixed up with these types. All for a couple of extra bucks. He'd liked them and they'd liked him, but when the crunch was on, just to save those couple of bucks, the "principles of sound business," they'd thrown him to the wolves. They'd ruined him.

Here he was sticking his neck out for them again, and, if he thought about it, he'd probably find out he'd fought the Pusan Perimeter for them.

The real question was: Were they worth it? Had he fought Pusan so some guy could sell a beer? Had he gotten wiped out in Chicago so some guy could sell a car?

That brought him around to now, to Eros Ranch. Before he could even think about it, he threw down the bourbon. It was his fourth on an empty stomach. He felt his head growing light. All the sensations in his body seemed to focus in his eyes. Thinking of Eros, he flushed with heat.

Do what you have to do and we'll back you, Pete Lockwood had said to him this morning. Well, he had done something. Now let's see what happens. He rubbed his giant paw across his brow. He faced the fear that he'd been plagued with all his life: that he wasn't particularly smart. Whenever he talked to superiors or to those business types, he felt he tried to make up in brusqueness what he lacked in thought. He had brawn, and plenty of guts, but he always felt outclassed in the brain department.

Maybe he played the patsy again. He didn't have that much time to think about the handling of the Eros situation. Mayor Lockwood wanted an immediate decision and, by God, got one. Maybe it wasn't the brightest, but it was the most direct. Maybe it would work. Lots of things worked—if you had the right backing. Everything was riding on his decision—one he knew he would live to regret. Lockwood had talked about state prosecutor for next year. "Hell, Anton, after all the publicity the feast brings us, you'll be in line for sure." Was it possible?

He got scared when he thought that the plan might be all air. He knew he had to take it step by step, deal with problems as they arose. If only he'd had more time to think it through.

Harry bought the next bourbon. "Good health, Tony," he said as he laid it on the table.

"Thanks." For the first time, the sheriff's lips formed a faint smile.

Moving his drink upward toward his lips, Whitney's wrist brushed his badge. He let his wrist linger against the metal. He thought about the badge as a symbol of all the things he thought good in life. A cop. A law enforcement agent. A guy who fought crime, protected the helpless. The Blue Knight. Why did things get so confused?

Long John and Big Jim ducked into the living room to find the lights out and the occupants crouched down behind pieces of furniture.

"That was good thinking, turning out the lights, but you can put them back on. You can get up, too. Looks to me like there ain't going to be any shooting as long as we stay in the house."

Long John and Big Jim looked out the darkened window for a minute then switched on the lights.

"Let's see if we're right," he said.

The crouchers, especially Costaign, seemed embarrassed in the merciless blast of light. They stood slowly. They were silent at first, then a babble of questions boiled from them.

"What *was* it?"

"Who are they?"

"Why are they shooting at us?"

The group crowded around Big Jim and Long John at the window for a moment. Obviously correct in their surmise that they were safe as long as they remained indoors, Big Jim and Long John stood a long time at the windows. The others drifted back to their divans. They were so full of tension it dripped from the tips of their fingers.

"I don't understand," Pat said. The unaccustomed sound of panic in her voice caused the others to look at her. "I really don't understand. It's incredible. Twenty-nine people die. We come up to make a routine investigation. Then the sheriff disappears. The police won't let us through their roadblock. They force us to stay here. Then somebody starts shooting at us. I don't understand. And I'm scared."

The others in the room shared Pat's fears but said nothing. Costaign, who knew of her fierce independence, made no move to comfort her. Instead he walked to the two men at the window.

"I guess I must have looked pretty silly hiding behind the couch," he said, with a sour grin.

"You ain't stupid," said Big Jim, without turning. "Behind the couch is a good place to be when the shit starts flying."

"Know what they call a guy who hides behind a couch?" Long John asked. "A survivor."

In a strange way, Costaign resented their casual acceptance of his act. They were both combat veterans. They knew how they would act in a time of danger. Costaign saw his hiding as an act of cowardice and was ashamed. He tried to assuage his shame by moving up with Long John, facing the window openly, with no protection between him and the guns.

"I wonder who they are," Costaign said.

"Beats the shit out of me," said Big Jim.

"Am I crazy? They couldn't be the police up there, could they? If the sheriff didn't want us to leave, that would be a good way to keep us here. But that's insane. Police don't do things like that. Shooting at people."

"Beats the shit out of me," Big Jim repeated.

At the word *police*, Pat stood from her chair. "Why didn't I think of that before," she said. "If the phone has been routed into the sheriff's office, all we have to do is dial. He'll have somebody out here to take care of this."

"Like he's taken care of everything else," Costaign said, almost under his breath.

"The phone's dead, I'm telling you," said Candy.

Pat disappeared behind the drapes into the bar.

"Man, I don't know no cops got automatic weapons," said Long John, "least for a scene like this."

"Then who are they?" said Costaign.

"They ain't cops. I ain't a guy gives cops no medals, you know," Big Jim said, "but these guys are sumpin' else. I never met no cop stupid enough to go around shooting at citizens. Specially at doctors, when one of them works for the state health department."

"Who else but the police wants to keep us here?" Irene asked from her position on the divan.

"I don't know," Big Jim answered.

"If they're not police, how come the deputies on the roadblock didn't hear the gunfire and come up to check it out? I know the roadblock is quite a distance, but in this silence gunfire like that should travel."

"I don't know that either. I *do* know there's more than one way to skin a cat. You got any thoughts, long fellow?"

Again the others fell silent. Long John and Big Jim seemed to have naturally assumed the roles of strategy planners.

"Yeah, I guess. I know we ain't staying here. Seems to me if you and me was to get to our car, we could make a run for it, if we keep them trees between us and them. Come back with them chicken-shit deputies. Leave the others in the house till we get back," Long John said.

"Wait a minute, there," Big Jim said. "If I was trying to pin some people in a house I'd have guns *all* around the house, not just in front of it. Maybe the only guns we saw were the ones out front."

"There it is," said Long John.

"Look," said Costaign. "My car is parked in the garage. Why don't you hop into it and rush out to yours? It would give you some protection. For that matter it's smaller, less of a target. You could make a run in it, instead of yours."

"That's good thinking, Doc," said Big Jim. "Only thing is, if we use your car to get to ours, we'd lose a lot of time switching from one to the other, and them hardcores out there could tag us. If we're going to make a run, the Caddy's got speed and pickup. What we need is some kind of diversion to give me and the lank here a chance to make a shot at it."

Upset and disappointed, Pat put the phone receiver back in its cradle. Candy had been right all along. The line was dead.

Pat felt disoriented. She had been the authority in all the jobs she had handled for the health department so far, and people around her had been deferential. Here, at Eros Ranch, something had gone wrong. The situation had already reached the point, and seemed to be getting deeper, where her "authority" was meaningless.

She wondered how Bob felt. She'd noticed that he, too, seemed to be floundering. Suddenly, she felt close to him.

"I want to go with you," Costaign said to Big Jim and Long John, trying to atone for his feeling of cowardice, having been found cringing behind the divan.

"No, Doc. We're used to working together. 'Preciate the offer, but I think we'd be able to move faster alone. Besides, we need somebody to stay here and take care of the broads," said Big Jim.

"You make it sound as though you two were raised in a shooting gallery," said Irene from the background.

Big Jim guffawed, breaking the tension between himself and Costaign.

"Not exactly. But we been kicking around the ashcans for a couple of years."

Again the conversation became a private planning session between the two old friends.

"This diversion you were talking about. What did you have in mind?" Long John asked.

"I don't know. I was figuring though that whoever is doing the shooting is probably men. Now, I was also thinking maybe they been out in the desert for a while. What would it take to distract a man who'd been out in the desert?"

"Long John smiled. "Candy?" he asked.

"Why not?"

"I don't understand," said Costaign.

"Okay, Doc, look. Me and long fellow here have to get to the convertible while there's still a bit of light out there. We could wait till it gets pitch dark, turn out the lights in the house, and make a run for it. Chances are we'd make it to the car all right, but we'd probably kill ourselves getting through the trees. The only way we could do it would be to turn the car's lights on, and one minute after that we'd be blown-away mothers. Dig?

"On the other hand, if we can get to the car while there's *just* enough light to see by, we can get to the access road without turning the lights on. It might be just dark enough to screw up their aim. Now in order for us to get from here to there we got to have something that'll take their minds off us for just the couple of seconds we need."

Costaign nodded.

"Hey, Candy. Come here a minute will you?" said Long John. "How you feeling? Better?"

"Sure," said the young woman. "Lots better. Why?"

Big Jim explained. "Think you're up to being our diversion?"

The idea frightened the woman; there was also something about it that made her smile. "If I can't, who can?" she said slowly.

Pat had returned from the bar. "Now wait a minute, you two, you can't risk that woman's life like that. If you need a diversion, there must be a better way."

"I don't think there's a better way, ma'am," Big Jim said, placing his hand on Candy's shoulder. "Nobody's gonna put a slug in a woman, especially one that looks like Candy. Give Candy sixty seconds and she'll make those dudes forget they got guns in their hands."

Candy beamed under Big Jim's approval.

"He's right," said Irene to Pat. Then to the men she said, "Why don't you guys let me do it. Candy may still be shaken up. I may not have Candy's figure, but I guess I can attract a man."

"Bullshit," said Long John with such vehemence it caused Big Jim to look at him. "I mean . . ."

"Too skinny?" Irene said ironically.

"It's not that . . ."

Her pride stung, Candy said, "No way. I may not be as cool as you are. I can pull my load though."

"Sure you can, hon. I didn't mean . . ." Irene began.

Candy turned haughtily to Big Jim. "What do you want me to do?"

Big Jim smiled. "You know *what* to do. Think you can do it right about now?"

Candy nodded. The fear she had swallowed lay like a cheap meal in her stomach.

"Okay, let's do it," said Big Jim.

For one second, Long John's eyes locked with Irene's. The tall man tried to understand his feeling of a moment ago. He turned then and strode away.

A minute later, stereo disco music roared out over the lawn, and Long John returned. "That'll give you something to play with," he said to Candy. He was also carrying a bucket. "Now be sure you go to the fountain on the right-hand side of the house. The one opposite the Spanish fountain. Take this with you. Make them think you're going to get water or something."

The group moved away from the main windows lest an observer psyche out their plot. The terror began to chalken Candy's face. She looked like a child who had taken a terrifying dare and could think of no way out.

"Break a leg," said Irene smiling.

"You just watch me," Candy said bravely.

She headed toward the door with a firm step. She put her hand on the knob and stopped. She turned to smile again at the group, and then, in a single burst of courage, she opened the door and dashed out.

When it slammed behind her, each person held his breath waiting for the gunfire. They heard Candy's steps work their way across the porch. The group returned, kneeling, to the windows. They peered over the sills. Candy was on the lawn. The last few seconds had worked a miraculous change in her. She was no longer the frightened child. Swinging her hips, throwing her shoulders back so that her breasts stood out boldly, she strolled nonchalantly toward the fountain on the right.

"What'd I tell you, man," said Long John.

Pat, uncharacteristically, turned from the windows and began to sob.

Costaign touched her shoulder. "She'll be all right."

When Pat looked up her eyes were red and deep set. "No, she won't, Bob. None of us will." Again, she broke into sobs. There was no way to explain to him that her sixth sense was raking her spine like a penknife.

CHAPTER
SEVEN

Now that the late twilight sky seemed clamped over it like a scarlet lid, the gulley was dark. The hill behind the mobile homes was not to be seen from the hacienda; even the eucalyptus grove was a gray-on-black smear with broken teeth gaping upward toward the lightness. Candy's body, as she walked, seemed to exhude an unnatural paleness, a wraithlike transluc-ence.

"You about ready to cut out?" Long John asked, taking his eyes from the sobbing woman doctor.

"Say when," Big Jim answered.

The two men were tense as Candy neared the foun-tain. The house lights fell on her; the frenzied, wailing moans from the stereo blared. Candy walked catlike and gracefully the last few steps and placed the bucket down on the rim of the fountain. Every eye was fixed on her as a slow, sensuous dance took hold of her body. At first, she snapped her fingers and moved her hips in a gentle circular motion. With her head thrown back, Candy swayed with the beat as if she were in a trance, overcome with abandon.

From the hill came no sound. And no shooting.

She danced her way around the fountain, slowly and sinuously. When she was on the far side, in full view of the men on the hill, she turned her back to them. Still in rhythm, she stroked her hips and breasts. The night throbbed with sexual excitement as the record abruptly ended. Candy stood motionless, breathing heavily.

Again the music, again the movement and stroking. In a teasingly slow graceful motion, her back still to the hill, Candy lifted her dress over her head and threw it away. In her panties and bra, both incredibly brief, she continued her weaving, her hands continued their explorations, only this time on bare flesh.

Katie and Irene watched from the window: two professionals admiring another's cameo performance. Pat was embarrassed. She wanted to take her eyes away, but, she too, was fascinated by Candy's movements and gyrations. For an instant, she was not a doctor, but a woman. She had a quick fantasy seeing herself in Candy's place.

Candy danced another full circuit around the fountain. Returning to the spot in view of the hill, she again turned her back and coyly removed both final pieces of clothing. The whiteness of her nude body made her seem even more ghostly. She seemed part of the night and the hills and the trees, a throbbing lost child of nature who had at last been recovered, and who now offered herself to the very earth from which she had been created.

"Stand by," said Big Jim. "Cotton Mather would be distracted by this time."

"I ain't doing so bad myself," Long John answered.

Big Jim's mouth tightened. His body crouched. "Go right over the porch rail onto the grass. We'll go doubled over."

The music moved toward a crescendo. The figure of Candy whirled with passionate intensity and increasing speed.

"Get ready," Big Jim whispered.

Suddenly, Pat screamed.

Costaign's eyes flared open to the size of quarters. He tried to point with an arm turned to wood. Then he yelled, "Look! Holy Jesus!"

In that moment, everyone in the house was frozen with horror.

What had seemed to be a wave of utter blackness reared up from the darkness of the hillside beyond the mobile homes and washed down into the compound. The rolling wave might have been lava or boiling tar. It roared as if a billion billion leaves were being driven before a hurricane. So loud was the roar, so terrified the people in the hacienda, that they couldn't hear the masculine bellowings from the hillcrest.

The wave moved so quickly that poor Candy, rapt in

her own sensuous dance, naked and vulnerable, had only time to turn toward the sudden roaring, and it was upon her! It immediately buried her to the knees and flowed on!

Her shrieks and howls were lost in the roaring. She thrashed and spun and whirled! She tore at her body with her hands, her fingers crooked like talons! She tried to kick, but her feet were hopelessly and nightmarishly mired! Each second, the tide rose higher. A coating of black suddenly flowed up over her naked flesh! She became a maddened animal! She clawed and ripped her own flesh! She tried to run! She was immediately blinded by a stream of blackness that shot upward and clung to her face! The thigh-high blackness bound her legs like molasses! She lunged forward, screaming in panic, and toppled face first into the morass! She was seen no more.

At the hacienda, there was only madness, expressed in screams, too. They knew what the wave was.

Cockroaches!

Trillions of roiling, bubbling, seething, crawling, slithering, scratching cockroaches!!

The wave, having engulfed the grounds, raced toward the house. It had already begun to climb the porch when Costaign, the first to regain his wits, began shouting over the hurricane roar.

"The garage! Get to the garage!"

He slapped and pushed his companions to unfreeze them. By the time the first trickle entered beneath the door and spread like an ink stain across the floor, the six terrified people were dashing for the kitchen. "Keep going! Keep going! Get to the garage!" Costaign continued screaming. They fled past the walk-in refrigerator with its dead stacked like cordwood inside. A few feet away, in the garage, they found Costaign's VW. "Get in. Quick," Costaign shouted, as he flung open the door. "It's watertight. It'll keep them out!" Thank God he hadn't locked the doors this morning!

The six piled into the car like chipmunks into their burrow, their screams filling the confined space as much as their bodies. Frantic bodies twisted and writhed, tearing their clothing. They were no longer creatures of convention: They were terrified human souls clawing for survival against a horror beyond imagination. Costaign, the last in, slammed the door behind him!

No sooner had he done so, than the first gush of roaches rolled out through the kitchen door. They spread out across the floor like swamp water. The tide, coming so fast now that it jammed up on itself in the doorway like floodwater trying to escape from a control channel, soon became a solid black, abysmal ghastliness, spewing itself at the car!

The first of the roach bodies rattled against the car like sleet. The roar, contained indoors, doubled in intensity. Like the inky, fetid tide of the river Styx, the black mass of roaches rose. First to the hubcaps, then to the fenders, then to the door handles, finally, in an instant of unspeakable horror, to the windows. Millions of feelers wiggling, mandibles mawing, faces, legs, and shiny bellies pressed against the glass in full view of the stricken occupants!

The car itself rocked under the impact of the assault. There was no screaming now. Only the tense, breathless wait for the first roach to appear within the car.

"Get this sumbitch out of here!" Long John bellowed over the roar. "We'll plow through!"

Costaign, sitting behind the wheel, used every nerve in his body to keep himself together. He worked the key into the ignition and turned it. The engine chugged for a moment, then caught, in a roar. Costaign rammed the stick into reverse and eased off the clutch. The car groaned backward.

"No! No!" Long John shouted. "Forward! Not back!"

The engine sputtered and died.

"Shit," Big Jim shouted.

After the noise of the engine, the roar of the roach tidal wave seemed even louder.

"Christ, they must have filled the exhaust pipe," Costaign called. "The whole thing must be stuffed with them!"

The devil tide now held the helpless car at its mercy. There were no longer any thoughts within the car, only the tiny, flickering flames of human life submerged in a metal coffin in a sea of ebony death. Their eyes were wide. Their breaths were grunts. Their fists clenched. Their flesh frigid, yet bathed in sweat. Their minds no longer functioned as mechanisms of cogent, linear comprehension. They existed only as recorders that absorbed sights and sensations, trying to sustain that flickering flame with resources unknown to the conscious mind.

There was no way for the occupants of the car to judge the passage of time. Soon, however, as such things are measured, each person found himself sucking deeply for breath, succeeding only in drawing streams of hot moisture which seared the lungs.

"The air's getting bad," Costaign said, at last. "We can't stay here. There's no way to open the vents."

"What about the air conditioner?" Katie gasped from the back seat.

"No good," said Costaign. "We have to have the engine on."

"You're right, Doc. The air ain't going to last much longer," said Long John. "We got to do something, quick. We can't stay here. How the hell do we get out? We don't know how long them roaches are going to be around."

"Probably till morning. Till it gets light again," said Costaign.

"We'll never last that long. Even if we get out, where the hell do we go?" Long John said.

"What about the refrigerator in the kitchen?" Irene asked. "It's only right over there. If we could get inside it, the roaches couldn't get at us."

It no longer mattered that the refrigerator was filled with bodies. Such niceties of civilized conduct are not for those hanging onto the brink of extinction.

"That's good thinking," said Long John, "but how do we get there?"

"Bet your ass it's good thinking," said Big Jim. "We sure as shit have to do something fast. Man, I can't breathe. I got an idea. It may be dangerous, but, Jesus Christ, look at us now. We're dead one way or the other. Want to try it?"

His five companions shuddered when Big Jim told them his plan. So numb had they become to everything but simple survival, no one disagreed. They had to try anything.

Long John and Big Jim scrunched themselves down onto the floor of the front seat. While Costaign pressed himself against the driver's door to give them more room, Long John and Big Jim, with tools passed to them out of the back-seat well, began digging into the floorboards.

"Don't make no holes those fucking bugs can get through," Long John cautioned.

"Man. I'll try not to. We want to get to the trunk not to the ground."

At first breakthrough, each man held his breath, lest the trunk be filled with roaches. A Phillips screwdriver in hand, Big Jim, the stronger of the two, worked his full arm through the hole they had created. He located the gas tank. With murderous slashes, he punctured it in half a dozen places. The already heavy air was permeated with the stench of gasoline.

"God, I hope we're doing the right thing," said Costaign, making it sound prayerful.

"Ain't nothing else we can do," said Big Jim, pulling his arm back out. "Good thing we're a couple of feet uphill from the kitchen door. All the gas'll flow under the roaches downhill. All we got to do now is wait till the tank is good and empty."

"Everybody ready?" Long John asked, looking into all the stricken faces.

Big Jim ignited an entire pack of matches and shoved it through the hole. He withdrew his arm so quickly that he tore bloody streaks in it from the jagged edges.

From the trunk came a long, soft sigh. As it ended, a blinding orange and blue fireball whooshed up around the VW. They couldn't see it from inside, but the river of gas that had flowed downhill behind them burst upward and moved toward the entrance way like a flow of glowing lava. A flash of heat jolted the inside of the car. The sea of cockroaches, now confronted with horrible death itself, ebbed away.

"Go!" Big Jim shouted.

Long John pressed the handle and smashed his shoulder into the door. Even with the thinning of roaches the fire had caused, he could only open it about two feet. He was suddenly deluged by flames and roaches. He hurled himself into the morass, screaming like a madman.

One by one, fear stricken beyond reason, the others followed.

The weight of the roaches' bodies had muffled the worst effects of the flames. Hundreds of thousands of roach bodies had sizzled and crisped in the fire that would give a chance of life to their enemies. Leading the way, the others shrieking and writhing behind, Long John, in several giant steps, sloshed through the burning roaches.

Reaching the refrigerator door, he ripped at it with all his wild strength and again succeeded in creating only a narrow opening. His partners, wailing, bellowing, crying, thrashing, one by one, squeezed through! Like burrs, thousands of unburned insects clung to them and swarmed into the refrigerator with them!

After Big Jim slammed the door behind them, the clear boundary line between this world and the dark, keening universe of insanity was no longer visible in the refrigerator. Six human remnants, their ragged clothing burned or torn away by their own hands, their skin charred, crammed into a confined place with twenty-nine rigid corpses, pressed so closely that the flesh of the living and the flesh of the dead were almost indiscernible. Like wild men of Bedlam they hacked and stamped and slashed and battered the roaches that had followed them in! It was a scene of madness, screaming, and flailing arms!

When, at last, all the roaches were dead, one by one, the humans dropped to the floor in exhaustion. They gasped and choked in their cage of death. Their crawling enemies were dead now, only they remained alive. Alive and entombed, as though they lay in their open graves waiting for the first shovel full of dirt to fall.

The temperature of the refrigerator had been set at forty degrees. Each of the six, panting, alone with his own shattered brain, pressed his face against the coolness of the wooden floor planking. It eased their pains. It supplied the single connection with the world they had known. One by one, they gave up. Their minds unable to bear more, they dropped off into the mercy of sleep.

||||||||||||||||||||||||||||||||||||||||||||||||||||||||||||||||||||||||||||||||||||||

CHAPTER
EIGHT

Oooo-wheee! What a slit!

Banzo had grinned broadly as he watched the chick strut over to the fountain with the bucket in her hand. Man, if that's the kind of gear they got in that stash, what the hell were they shooting for? Looking at her, Banzo wriggled his feet in the sand and lifted himself on his elbows, removing his cheek from the stock of the M-16. His position suddenly seemed inadequate. Military fashion, he worked his way on his belly closer to the rim of the canyon. It was an instinctive move. He had been in the slam almost a week without so much as laying an eye on a broad, and suddenly his body was on fire.

Carmine, sprawled a few yards to his right, whistled

raucously. To his left, Cutter Brown whooped a Rebel yell. The woman in the pink dress was not oblivious to their admiration. Fucking-A she knew they were there. Watching her sure beat the shit out of waiting for them dudes to try making it to the car.

This whole scene was a lot better than what had been happening to them lately.

They were traveling. Seven of them: him, Cutter, Carmine, Boris, Ritter, Bird, and Patton. Down from 'Frisco. You know, just grooving. The cops in Vegas had said "split." So they split. Screw 'em. One thing you don't do is hassle a cop. That's strictly Hollywood, Marlon Brando shit. You wear club colors, man, and every cop in the world is looking for an excuse to bust your ass. Man, they stop you every three blocks. "We don't like your kind around here."

"What's *my kind*, man?" you want to say. "I'm an American citizen, right? You wanted *my kind* for your dragon-shit war." You don't say it, though. Give them an excuse and they grind the key up. You can't beat them bastards.

The Slavers had heard in Vegas about the big doings up at Cherakowa. Everything had been A-1 till that asshole in the pub. You don't screw with a *Slaver*. You lean on one, you lean on them all. So there was a little fight. Then in comes this rube sheriff. Next thing you know they were all slammed up. This sheriff—he's hip; he's nobody to screw with. He's got the juice to send you to Devil's Island, so they were all good boys.

One night, while they're waiting for their trial date,

the sheriff gets them all together and makes this crazy deal.

"You boys like to be on your way out of town in a week?" he says. "No questions asked?" Sure, man. All they got to do is use a couple of rifles to keep some people from leaving Eros Ranch, some kind of cathouse up in the hills. "You just keep 'em pinned. Nobody gets hurt. Next week, after the fiesta, you take off. Nobody says nothing."

Can you dig it! This sheriff wants to give *The Slavers* guns! How much can the sheriff protect them if the staties or the highway patrol come along? "No sweat," that crazy sheriff says, like he's John Wayne and this is Iwo Jima. "You boys do like I tell you, and you're on the road next week. If you don't want to, that's okay. Seems to me we had an armed robbery in town last week. There was six or seven guys involved."

"Shit, man, we weren't even in the state last week."

"Maybe you're wanted for something in California."

So what else is new?

They agree. The sheriff brings them to this old mining cabin way up in the sticks, stocks them with enough food and sauce, then brings them to this cliff over the cathouse. He stations the dudes at different places so that the pad is covered. It ain't a bad gig. In fact, it's an up. Like a game. Everytime somebody tries to leave the pad—whammo! Like them dudes this afternoon. The sheriff was even talking about laying a little coin on *The Slavers*.

Banzo and the other two had almost flipped when the

chick started to take off her dress. Man, that was real. Maybe they should have been taking care of business, but all they could do was watch her. The hooting had died down and each guy was left alone with his private fantasy.

Then . . .

Sheriff Whitney's phone rang a little after midnight. The bell pierced his head like a spear. Anxiety about his handling of the Eros Ranch affair had been swirling around his dreams like a carnival, so when the phone rang, he could hardly tell which was the dream and which the reality. The drinks he had thrown down on an empty stomach at Harry's had made his head a tender scab. His belly seemed filled with radioactive waste. He groaned as he reached for the receiver.

By the time he hung up, he knew his nightmare was continuing.

Jesus Christ. Trouble already. The sheriff swung his legs from under the blanket and reached for his clothes.

An hour later, he sat in one of the chairs drawn up around the splintery wood table in the deserted old miner's cabin. A single glass kerosene lamp sat in the middle of the table, dancing its light on the three rough faces around him. Beyond the ring of light, to the walls and corners of the cabin, darkness was thick and commanding.

"You bastards woke me up in the middle of the night and dragged me out here. You better have a good story! You didn't tell me shit on the phone."

The three faces remained immobile. Not so much that their owners chose them to be so, but rather through some inner restraint. Odd, the sheriff thought. Fear seemed the one quality these faces would not contain. They were all young and tough. One of the men wore a studded, battered leather jacket. The other two wore reinforced Levis. On the left breast pocket of each jacket, under a month's supply of dirt and grease, was a colorfully embroidered emblem of a fist dangling a chain, and beneath it the word *Slavers*.

"Well?" the sheriff insisted.

"Hey, man. It ain't like we don't appreciate the break you giving us, dig? What kind of motherfucking scene you got us into?"

"What the hell are you talking about? I got a head like a sore thumb and I don't feel like messing with you. I'd argue pretty goddam easy right now," the sheriff growled. "I work out a good deal for you birds, and the first time out you want to screw me up."

"Good deal? Fuck that 'good deal.' We done what we agreed. We didn't deuce out on you. But, man, you didn't say nothing about them fucking bugs either. They almost ate us alive. Ain't nobody in this club got shit in his blood. Man, I'll stand up to any sonofabitch in this world or jump Jesus. But I ain't screwing with a million frigging cockroaches."

"Cockroaches?" Whitney was puzzled.

"Cockroaches, man! Fucking millions of them!" Banzo, the bearded one, shouted.

"Are you going to tell me what you dragged me out here for, or am I going to toss your greasy ass back in the slam," the sheriff yelled.

"Jesus Christ, Sheriff! I'm telling you—cockroaches, man! Millions of them. All over the house. You know like the rattlesnakes that all come up from the ground in Arizona? Well, here it's roaches. And we're splittin'!"

Whitney's face was still a concrete wall. Banzo looked from the sheriff to his companions and back to the sheriff again.

"Okay, man. You want it, you got it!" He leaned over the table so he was face to face with him and laid the whole grisly story on Anton Whitney.

"Cockroaches?" the sheriff asked, after Banzo finished his nightmare description.

"Man, you never saw anything like it. Them bastards were crawling all over us. There must have been a billion of them!"

Roaches, the sheriff thought, and suddenly the events of the morning made sense to him. He could feel shudders ripple through him. Whitney looked like a man whose nightmares were coming true.

An hour later, Whitney was trudging alone through the dark mountains toward Eros Ranch. The cold white bar of his flashlight bobbled out in front of him. Horror gnawed at his belly. It was a time of night, alone in the mountains with the wailing wind, and the horror from his belly spread around him, growing like fungus.

He tried to visualize the details of the story those

biker creeps had told him. Cockroaches. Millions and millions of them. The gulley half-filled with them, like greasy coffee sloshing in a cup. This was the first horror. Now he was going back to that gulley. What would he find this time?

Whatever the bikers had told him, they believed. He remembered the last couple of minutes they were together in the cabin when he tried to talk them into going back with him.

"Fuck you, Jack!"

Banzo, the leader, had talked tough words, but the sheriff remembered the look on his face.

"No way. All deals are off. You ain't getting us back to that damn place. No way!"

"What the hell you think you're going to do?" Whitney asked.

"Look, man," Banzo began in unexpected terms of reconciliation, "give us a break. We did what you wanted. You got a whole different can of worms now. We'll just split and forget the whole thing. Whatta you say?"

An argument ensued, and Whitney had threatened to lock them up again. But he couldn't press it much because he had armed them. They held the M-16 on him and took off down the hill. He had chased them, even fired a couple of shots, but he knew he was outnumbered and had to let them go with a few curses and a couple of close zingers that merely caused them to move a little faster.

So they split, the sheriff thought, trudging through the dark. What the hell do I care about them? They're alley cats. As he drew closer to Eros, the prickling in his stomach grew more intense. He was going toward what had frightened a bunch of bad customers like them.

Good God. What had he done to those two docs?

CHAPTER
NINE

Morning came for the miserable occupants of the refrigerator, not as the normal transmutation of dawn to brassy daylight, but as a slowly awakening, dull awareness that life somehow still flickered here on the frontier of extinction. Surrounded by death, the air as chill as the grave, six sparks had managed to survive.

They stirred. Their skins were cold. Their joints ached. They did not look at each other, at first. Neither did they speak. They lifted themselves on pained elbows and knees, blind to the dead around them, ignoring the crunch of roaches.

They perceived with their nonvisual senses. The first thing they became aware of was the silence outside the door.

Pat's head, held between hunched shoulders, tilted first this way, then the other, listening like an animal. Her voice was a rasp. "Are they gone?"

"What time is it?" asked Costaign.

"Six-forty-five," Long John answered.

"They're gone," said Costaign. "At least they were by this time yesterday."

Big Jim, closest to the door, said, "It's quiet out there." He rose from the floor like a rusted puppet. He numbly pressed his weight against the plunger handle. Ponderously, the door swung open. Six tense pairs of eyes watched the slit of light spread wide like a verticle curtain.

They were gone.

Limping, numb, unspeaking, barely feeling, propping each other, they filed out of their tomb into the warm air, leaving with the roaches and the cordwood stack of corpses a little of their sanity, and a good part of their youth.

One by one, they made their way to the front porch, silently traversing the same route that last night had been a scene of howling madness. They sucked the cool, fresh air. Their skins drank the weak sunlight. Again they eased themselves to the floor.

Costaign looked out over the grounds. It was just about the same time of day as yesterday when he had first discovered Eros. Yesterday he had known fear, today he was beyond that. His fears had only been hints and forebodings. The worst had happened since then. He had survived. His body was not a peeled corpse.

Oblivion, peaceful and healthy, engulfed the six again. Sitting, lying, leaning, they dropped off to sleep. They might have fled, but their bodies could not think of tomorrow, they could only celebrate the life of the moment.

There was a sluggish movement in the deep body of the earth. A billion tunnels, running like veins and capillaries, throbbed with slithering life. No longer boiling in passion now. Glutted. Fat. The individual corpuscles, feelered and mandibled, full-bellied with sacks of new life, seethed over and around each other, digging into the earth, breaking away from the veins, establishing places of reproduction. As they clawed, the breast of the earth shifted and moaned.

At the sheriff's office, Sergeant Emiliano Gomez wore the weight of his hours like a heavy coat. It was seven o'clock. The arrow-tipped hands of the old-fashioned clock above his desk seemed glued. The two-way radio next to him hummed with inactivity. The air was stale from his hours of cigarettes. He opened the top drawer of his desk idly, surveying the four pink telephone message slips. He stared for a few moments, then just as idly closed the drawer. He sighed. He leaned back in his chair, yawned, stretched his arms over his head. Afterward, he stuffed his shirt back into his belt. He blinked his heavy-lidded eyes.

Five past seven. Funny he should still feel so tired.

He'd usually pulled out of it by this time. Three to three-thirty was his bad time. It was impossible for him to keep his eyes open during that half hour. Unless, of course, something was happening. He thought of going home. His wife would be in a bathrobe. The two kids would have already gone off to school. She would make him a cup of tea. After all night on the desk, he would be coffeed out. He would take off his tie and belt equipment and feel ten pounds lighter. His wife would lock his gun up in the living room cabinet so the kids couldn't get at it. He would sit at the table talking to her, though she would still be bleary eyed. After two cigarettes she would ask him if he wanted breakfast. He would say no. Sometimes he would lead her by the hand to the bedroom. He would undress. She would throw her robe over a chair. In bed, they would respond quickly to each other. He would lie there sleepily. She would gather the robe around her.

"Why don't you stick around?" he would ask.

"You sleep. I've got things to do."

"You stick around, maybe I'll think of some things to do."

"You're bad." She'd smile.

"Bad—and good, maybe?"

"Maybe," she'd say. "I'll wake you before the kids come home."

"You always got something to do."

"That's right. And I'm always too tired to do them by the time you get done. Damn that night shift."

"Can't help it if I'm a morning man," he'd say.

"Go to sleep, baby. I'll wake you."

Gomez was getting excited thinking about his wife. In his mind he could see her naked hips. Man, how he loved those hips.

The door to the hallway pushed opened. It was Sergeant Deigan, his relief.

"What do you say, Gomez?"

"Not a hell of a lot. Glad you're in early. Got some shit to catch you up on."

Deigan filled his cup from a thermos. "Only decent coffee I can get around here." He joined Gomez at the desk.

"We been getting phone calls about Eros Ranch," Gomez said.

"From who?"

"People. Three relatives and a lawyer. All transferred up from Vegas PD. They're not sure their people went to Eros. The Vegas PD was scattering the calls to see if anybody'd heard of the missing people. You know how they do it."

"What'd you tell 'em?" Deigan asked.

"Nothing. Told them we'd look around. Told 'em the sheriff would be in later."

Deigan pulled up a chair.

"Man," he said, "I hope Whitney knows what the fuck he's doing."

"Yeah, me too," said Gomez.

Michael Boomer, eighteen, the all-night attendant at Peak-View Exxon Station, was tied hand and foot and lay sweating in the dark, stuffy confines of the locked closet. He had been kicking against the door until his legs had dropped in exhaustion. The stench of opened oil cans made breathing difficult.

Them bastards, he thought.

Beneath his anger, Boomer felt relief at being alive and unhurt. He had never known the feeling of staring down the barrel of a gun. Jesus Christ! When them *Hell's Angels*, or whatever they were, had stepped out of the darkness armed to the teeth with them Viet Nam kind of rifles he almost died. He was not about to mess with them.

He always thought those dudes were cool. But this gang looked like they were strung out. Like they'd been in a big hurry to get somewhere. He wondered, at the time, where they came from. Had they walked? Maybe. 'Cause the only thing they'd wanted was his car. With the guns and with that hurry-up look on their faces, man, they were welcome to it! They made him fill it up, while they kept looking over their shoulders like somebody might be after them. After tying him up and throwing him in this closet, they took off like big-assed birds.

Boomer guessed he had gotten off pretty easy. Those motorcyclists were supposed to be mean dudes. They hadn't hurt him, just tied him up and dumped him in this closet. He wondered where they were going in such a hurry. What had happened to their bikes? What'd they need his car for? Michael Boomer decided to wait quietly until Calvin relieved him at eight.

Irene was the first to stir. She sat up, supporting

herself against the wall under one of the windows. A
series of expressions, from terror to relief to cogni-
zance, followed the road her mind took to wakefulness.
She leaned back and closed her eyes. She felt no panic.
Now safe in the morning sun, her mind became a dry
beach that grasped only the knowledge that she was
safe. She opened her eyes and considered her companions,
as they lay around her.

As the sun warmed she began to notice the coolness
of the wind. She crossed her arms, and suddenly she
became aware that she was almost naked. For an
instant, a memory popped into her head and was
promptly repressed. In the refrigerator. The roaches.
The crawly feeling of their having worked their way
under her clothing. How she'd torn the clothing away
to be free of them. Everyone had spun like dervishes,
clawing at their own clothes.

The fleeting remembrance brought another vague
thought—the men on the hill last night. Were they
still there? Were they looking at her?

My God! she thought. Candy!

Irene lifted herself by bracing both palms flat against
the wall behind her. She staggered over to the rail. Her
movement caused Big Jim to open his eyes and stir.
She scanned the grounds by the fountain and a new
reality sunk in. A red, peeled, bloody blob stained the
morning grass. It neither moved nor breathed. A scum
of dead roaches formed a scab around what was left of
Candy.

The others on the porch were in various stages of

waking up. Irene turned away from Candy's body. Long John, his eyes on Irene, was sitting up.

"Candy?" he asked hoarsely.

"Uh-huh," Irene replied.

Long John said no more as Irene stepped across the porch and into the house.

Now, they were all awake and all too fully aware of what happened. Big Jim, Katie, Costaign, and Pat had each witnessed the carnage of yesterday morning, yet looking at Candy's one poor body, each seemed to focus on his own personal ordeal. Perhaps twenty-nine deaths are too diffused a thing to register any way but intellectually. In the agonized death of one brave woman, each had found his own agony, and perhaps his own salvation.

Soon they became aware of themselves, of their bodies and their spirits. They had almost recovered from the night, but they didn't quite know it. They looked to the hill and saw no gunmen. To the left, the way to the access road seemed clear, but nobody made a run. The four sat, or reclined, as though no other possibility existed.

Long John, standing alone, did not take his eyes from the door through which Irene had passed. His mind, still shuffling, tried to recall what sort of expression she had had on her face after viewing Candy's body. What was she in such a hurry for? What was she going to do to herself?

Long John hurried through the door. Standing at the base of the staircase, he called, "Hey, Renie! Hey, Renie! Where the hell are you?" He climbed the stairs, holding on to the banister. "Hey! Answer me, will you? Where are you?"

He ducked frantically into one room after the other, down the full length of the hall. When he found her, she was stepping out of a shower stall, dripping wet, with a towel in hand.

"I've been calling you. I guess you didn't hear me over the shower," he said. "I'm glad you're okay."

"I'm okay," she said dully.

"Sorry to bug you, but you scared hell out of me. I thought maybe you'd . . ."

Irene stopped toweling and looked at Long John. Her body remained in a frozen position; her face betrayed no emotion. Only her eyes moved. They raced back and forth over Long John's face with the speed of an electronic beam. His eyes were tender. His expression, concerned.

Inside Irene something melted, something long frozen into place. It flowed to her arms and legs, where it loosened her joints. It flushed color into her cheeks. It warmed her scratched and bruised body like the first sun after a long New England winter. Her features broke up like ice on a stream: first clicking, snipping, cracking, then a protracted sigh, followed by a final healthy gurgling.

Irene dropped the towel. Her eyes filled with tears.

"Oh, John," she said, softly, at first. "Oh, John. Oh, John!"

She half fell, half threw herself toward the tall man. His arms caught her and clamped her. Her sobbing, too, began softly, then burst all its restraints.

A curtained window looked out onto the early morning. The sun was turning gold, the wind was drifting through the trees.

The sun stretched across the sky, alone. The wind breathed into the treetops, alone. Each needed nothing but the other. Two humans, alone, and feeling their aloneness, needing one another for their survival.

"I'm all right now," Irene said.

"You sure?"

She had moved away from Long John's chest. She allowed herself, however, to remain in the clasp of the warm hands that held her shoulders. She seemed reluctant to take that final step away from him.

Long John's admiration for Irene's courage had grown after yesterday. Guts was his favorite virtue. Sooner or later it got down to pure balls. Once, in Nam, he had released a gook prisoner he should have blown away. That crazy bastard, alone, with one round in his ancient rifle, had sneaked in, blown four high-octane trucks, and had wanted to take on the whole goddam platoon with his bayonet. Couldn't kill a real hardcore sonofabitch like that. He deserved better.

Compared to Irene, that dude was a faker. Man, what a broad.

"I wish *I* could think of something to smile about," she said.

"I ain't smiling."

"You are."

"Okay, I am," he said. "I was just looking at all them bruises and scratches you got all over you. You look pretty shitty."

"You're not looking so groovy yourself," she said.

Long John realized he was shirtless, his chest a mass of purple welts. The right leg of his pants was ripped along the seam from ankle to hip. He'd lost his left shoe.

"I guess you're right," he said.

"Here," Irene said, as she bent over and undid the laces of the remaining shoe. Long John stood, allowing her to strip him. In a moment he was naked. She flinched at the sight of his wounds.

"Get in." She nudged him to the shower stall. Reaching around him, she adjusted the water temperature, then crowded into the stall with him. When the water was just right, she reached behind and closed the door.

"You taking another shower?"

"What's it to you? You paid your money, you get the service."

Irene handled the soap as though it were a sacramental item. She gently washed and massaged his flesh. She washed his chest in sweeping motions. Long John knew he was gaining strength from her, as she was from him. It seemed the ultimate in lovemaking.

"Did you find them?" Pat asked. She seemed as tense as a guitar string.

"Yeah," said Big Jim, "I found them. They're upstairs taking a shower."

"Are they all right? Did you see them?" she persisted.

"They're all right. I stuck my nose in the door, then bugged out."

"They've got the right idea," Costaign said. "We should be doing the same thing."

"Taking a shower together? How civilized," said Pat, with hostility.

"I mean, we should be getting these wounds cleaned out as soon as possible."

The four had gathered in the parlor.

"I know where we can get some clothes," Katie said.

All four stood in tatters. Pat had crossed her arms over her breast in an instinctive effort to hide her nudity.

"Why are we talking like this?" Pat said. "I don't want to stay here a minute longer than we have to. We can get washed and dressed and cared for in town. There's nothing to stop us if the gunmen are really gone."

"There's no rush now, Doc. We got a little slack," Big Jim said.

"Thank you very much for your professional opinion," Pat snapped.

"Ain't nothing gonna happen. We can go when we're ready," Big Jim said mildly.

Then, as if to belie his words, they heard heavy steps clump across the porch.

"Oh my God!" Katie whispered. "The gunmen are back! They've come after us!"

CHAPTER TEN

The sheriff, massive enough to blot out the sunlight, stood in the doorway. He shoved the door wide and entered as though he were plunging into cold water. When his eyes fell on Costaign, Symington, Big Jim, and Katie, he almost did a double take. His face turned to rock when he saw their tattered clothes, their wounds.

"Thank God, you're still alive," he said, in wonderment.

The four sighed with relief.

"Oh, Sheriff, thank God you're here," Pat barely breathed.

Big Jim, in one athletic bound, reached the sheriff and pumped his hand. "Man, I never thought I'd be so glad to see one of you people."

"Well, yeah—uh—I got here as soon as I could," said

Whitney. His eyes dwelled on Costaign guiltily, then tore themselves away. "I saw what happened."

There seemed to be a secret between the sheriff and Costaign. The other three were so overwhelmed by the sheriff's presence, they didn't notice.

"Well, I'm glad you're all okay. I'm Anton Whitney," he said, turning his shoulder on Costaign.

The three introduced themselves.

"The health department sent *you*?" Whitney asked.

"I'm a doctor, Sheriff," Pat responded coldly. "And now that you're here, we've got a lot of problems to handle."

Whitney's presence seemed to activate Pat. She instantly became all business, bringing the sheriff up to date on everything that had happened. Had he been in touch with her office? Had they asked about her? What had happened to the medical examiner's crew? They could forget the epidemic theory. Now they had to find out what was causing the abnormal reproduction in the roaches and how to stop it from spreading around the country.

Whitney was responding with a lot of uh-huhs and other short answers when Irene and Long John appeared on the stairs.

They were a strange sight. Stranger for the deadly serious circumstances. Long John wore a pair of pale blue silk pajamas, Irene a pair of pink shorts and a laced, slitted blouse. They grinned to see the sheriff and hurried down the remaining steps.

"The cavalry has arrived," Irene joked.

"You don't know how glad I am to see you, Sheriff," Long John offered.

Costaign could take no more. He stood up abruptly. "Sheriff, look . . ."

Whitney's head spun toward him. "We got some things to talk about—later," he cut in significantly. "First, I want all of you out of here. These two got the right idea about getting cleaned up and finding something to wear. We'll get you some decent clothes in town. I want this place closed up as soon as possible."

Though Pat had some questions, as did the others, about taking the time to clean up there when they could be in Cherakowa in a few minutes, the sheriff seemed their angel of liberation and they would have listened to him if he'd asked them to stand on their heads. Pat, Katie, and Big Jim headed upstairs, leaving Long John, Irene, and Costaign with the sheriff.

"The doc and me got some medical things to talk about," Whitney said. "Why don't you two—uh . . ."

"Long John Markley. She's Irene Ludlow."

"Well, yeah—Long John."

"We'll put together some coffee, if we can find any," said Irene.

Long John and Irene hoped the sheriff and Costaign would talk about more than "medical things." There were a lot of questions that had to be answered. Where had the gunmen come from? How come the shots hadn't been heard by the roadblock? Hadn't there been inquiries about the girls who worked at Eros Ranch? Or the customers? What about the people who usually made service deliveries, hadn't they wondered why they weren't allowed in?

Irene and Long John went into the kitchen. The sheriff and Costaign went into the bar. The sheriff poured two bourbons. The sheriff called Irene and handed her a couple of bottles.

"Here," he said, "give the coffee a good lacing with this. You guys look like you could use it."

Down at the access road, the wind jiggled a eucalyptus tree. The tree stood out from the high shoulder that bordered the road. A brown leaf on one of the branches bent under the wind for a second, then snapped loose. It swam out over the road as long as the wind lasted, then spun downward. It landed, curled up around its central rib, like a beached canoe, exactly on the line where the tar of the road met the soil. It edged over and finally came to its rest.

A tiny whirlpool of earth began beneath it. The earth continued to fall away until the leaf was lying in a miniature swale. The surface, unable to support itself against the burrowing of a trillion roaches, was beginning to cave in on itself. There were so many tunnels that this was only the start of collapse. Soon the surface of the earth would be unrecognizable.

"Man, that fucking dude is unwrapped," Cutter said to Boris as they brought up the rear of the column *The Slavers* formed, working their way through the mountains back to Eros Ranch. The "dude" under discussion was Banzo, their leader.

"I never seen him so pissed," Boris answered.

"I don't blame him. I'm kinda pissed myself. Man, that sheriff is a slimy bastard. Can you dig his pulling a thing like that? Making like he's working a deal with us. Sure, you do this for me and I'll do that for you. Then giving it out on the radio that we escaped and were dangerous, and like every cop in the state should keep his eye out for us. Man, we never asked for his fucking deal!"

"Yeah," said Boris, "and it's a goddam good thing we boosted that kid's car with the police radio in it, otherwise we'd of walked right into it. Them gas station dudes use it to hear the cops tell about accidents so they can hustle on over for a little business. Can you dig what would've happened if we hadn't heard it before some pig picked us up?"

"Right on," said Cutter. "Jesus, I wish Banzo'd take it easy with this hiking. My poop is dragging."

"Like you say, man, the dude is pissed. I never seen him this mad, but I don't know what I think about offing a pig. A sheriff, too. That's bad news. You off a citizen, that's bad enough. You off a pig, they don't stop till they get you," said Boris.

"I think Banzo's flipped. He came out of that Viet Nam war wacky. I don't like getting fucked over by that sheriff either, but, hey, this is wild."

"I think you're right about the war. But Banzo goes ape shit whenever he sees a uniform, anyway," said Boris.

"Bet your ass I am. I knew him before he went. He was a tough dude, but he wasn't no nut."

Cutter and Boris could not ease the knot of tension in their stomachs. Killing a sheriff is bad business. Radio or no radio, right now they should be splitting the state fast.

Sgt. Gomez finished briefing Sgt. Deigan, and both were edgy. Each felt the nervous desire to move, to stretch, to walk, yet their jobs in the office forbade it. They were the only two the sheriff had taken into his confidence about the Eros affair and they were nervous about it. A dangerous game. If anything went wrong, it could cost them their jobs. But they had to back Whitney. He was a hell of a guy. A tough sonofabitch, all right, but the best boss they ever had. He gave you no bullshit as long as you did your job. There also had been the matter of favors. Whitney was responsible for their promotions.

When Gomez thought this, he felt a twinge of guilt. Maybe to Deigan it was a matter of simply loyalty. After all, he was an Anglo. To Gomez it was a deep personal commitment to Whitney, to the man who had given him what damned few others would have. Gomez did not fool himself. The only reason he had been appointed to the force under old Sheriff Cranston had been the federal guidelines. No Chicano had been in the sheriff's department in this county before.

Then Whitney had come along after the old man retired. It did not matter a damn to Whitney that Gomez was a Chicano. When promotions came around, that big sonofabitch had only looked at the guy's service record. Gomez had become the first Mexican-

American in Arapahoe County to wear sheriff's sergeant stripes. You had to stick with a guy like Whitney.

"You don't have to take over the desk yet. It's only seven-thirty," Gomez said.

"I'm here. What the hell. I might as well do something," Deigan answered.

"If you're going to stay, then I'll see if I can find the boss and check with him," he said, picking up the phone.

Gomez dialed Eros Ranch. He hung up.

"That's funny," he said, after trying twice more. "Sounds like the line's out."

"So what? The boss probably arranged it."

"It's funny, that's all."

"The boss knows what he's doing," Deigan said.

Soon the sheriff's office was rattling with the sound of shift change. Footsteps and voices reverberated in the dull air of the hallway. The new people seemed to bring the freshness of morning in with them. The night people were heavy with time.

"*Mamacita* is waiting for me," Gomez said as he waved goodbye to Deigan over his shoulder.

"Okay, buddy. See what you can do about getting in touch with the boss, will you?"

"Sure. I'll take a little ride before I go home."

Gomez climbed in his car. What the hell. How long would it take him to check with the guys on the roadblock. Maybe I'll stop off at Eros, he thought.

"I thought you guys were just going to have a quiet night out here. I swear to you, Doc, I never felt you would be in any danger," the sheriff said, alone with Costaign in the bar.

The one drink sat heavily in Costaign's stomach. Its warm fingers tickled the backs of his eyes and the base of his brain. He felt he was seeing two Whitneys. One was a man holding guilt inside him like a sick dog. No doubt the sheriff had never intended harm for either himself or Pat, or the others that at the time he knew nothing about. But the other was a scared man telling him some fairy tale. The sheriff claimed, he had been distracted by the escape of seven motorcycle gang members from the county jail. He had thought it would be a simple matter of assigning a couple of men to the job, but one thing had led to another until he had come out to Eros last night to find it buried in cockroaches.

The whole story was wrong somehow.

"At least we know where the cyclists went when they left the jail," said Costaign ironically. "Can I get you another one of these deadly bourbons. They're tasting pretty good, at this point."

"No thanks, Doc. So you think it was the motorcycle gang that kept you pinned down?"

"Why not?"

"I guess you're right. You say they had automatic weapons?" the sheriff asked.

"Long John and Big Jim said they did. M-16s. They ought to know. They're our resident experts in heroics."

"I wonder where they got them?" said the sheriff, as though in deep thought.

"Maybe they enlisted," said Costaign.

The sheriff gave Costaign a long, hard look. He stood

up from the bar stool and walked to the window. After
a moment's hesitation, he turned, faced Costaign, and
walked slowly back to his original position. He was a
man making a decision.

"Doc—uh—look. We've only known each other a day
now, and that ain't a long time, as getting to know
someone goes. We been through some things together.
And maybe going through some things together makes
you get to know a person a lot faster. If you know what
I mean."

"I think I do," said Costaign.

"Okay. I need a friend right now, Doc. Couple of years
ago in Chicago, I got myself in a jam. Nothing crimi-
nal, or like that, but a jam. I felt like I couldn't trust
nobody. Maybe that was a mistake. That same thing
could be happening right now. This time it could be
worse. Goddam thing's got out of my hands. Maybe I'm
right and maybe I'm wrong, but I got a feeling I can
trust you. Maybe I gotta trust you. You're young, but
you seem pretty savvy. There's some things I got to tell
you. Maybe you ain't going to like 'em. Maybe this is
the worst mistake I ever made. Anyhow, here goes."

When Whitney finished his explanation, Costaign
looked as though he had been hit with a club. He sat
back, facing away from the bar, his drink held in his
lap in the loose grip of both hands.

"That's the whole story, Doc." The sheriff sat tensely
waiting for Costaign's reaction, yet he seemed relieved
to have expelled the noisome secret.

"Christ. It's insane," Costaign said, at last.

"I know it is," said the sheriff. "Maybe you do some

dumb things when you get over forty-five and you're
worried about your job. The mayor kind of spooked me,
and I got things going before I really had a chance to
think about them. I don't know. Maybe I made a mistake telling you all these things. It's just that when I
saw this place with all them roaches, I knew that there
were things more important than saving my job. And
that's no shit. I didn't know how bad things were going
to get. How could I have known about them roaches? I
wouldn't have asked you and the other doc and them
other people to go through that.

"All I'm asking is for you to go along with me for a
while and I'll get this whole thing straightened out.
There's no sense in more people getting hurt."

"You mean, if we tell a lot of lies," Costaign said.

"Come on, Doc. Don't talk like a college kid. Didn't I
just spill my guts to you? I'm telling you we can
backtrack and nobody gets hurt. You know I'm being
straight with you. There just ain't no sense in tearing
the world down if you don't have to."

"Nobody gets hurt? What about the motorcyclists?
They get hurt," said Costaign.

"Oh, fuck them. They're alley rats. That's all. Look
what they tried to do to you. You give a shit about
punks like that?"

"No they're not 'alley rats.' They're human beings
just like us."

The sheriff looked at Costaign as though he couldn't
believe the doctor's ingenuousness. "No, they ain't.
They're animals. You don't know them the way I do.

What difference does it make, anyhow? By this time they're three hundred miles from here."

Costaign's anger rose. "What about Candy Ackerman? That woman out on the lawn. Can you fix it with her, too?"

"I swear to God, Doc. I didn't know anything like this was going to happen. Don't you think I feel bad enough about it? What do you want, my fucking blood? I can't bring her back to life. If I could, I would. Doc, I came to you as a friend and told you the truth. I could have lied to you, but I didn't. I ain't crawling and I ain't taking no shit from you. You either understand what I'm telling you or you don't."

Before the conversation could go any further, the other five inhabitants of the hacienda trooped into the bar, dressed in as bizarre an assortment of clothes as one might find in a brothel. They carried coffee cups and glasses. The sheriff glared at Costaign. Costaign was glad for the interruption.

Whitney began talking to the newcomers. They tried to kid about the clothes, but the jokes fell flat. Costaign leaned his back against the bar and slugged down the bourbon, then promptly poured himself another.

Again he was plagued with his feeling of inadequacy. What should he do with the sheriff? Go along? Or denounce him? On one hand, Whitney had done some pretty terrible things. But then, he was as human and scared as the rest. It would be easy to go along with the sheriff. Would it be right? If he fought him, would it be worth it?

There it was. Indecision. It seemed a part of his life. He had taken this vacation to do a little thinking about the Sunburst Hotel. Here he was in the outside world and he seemed lost. Was that why he kept working at the hotel? To avoid decisions?

"All right," the sheriff said, taking a last look at Costaign, "you people all set. Let's get the hell out of here. We got a lot of things to do today. How about you, Doc? You ready?"

"I'm ready," Costaign said.

CHAPTER
ELEVEN

As they crunched the grounds, their freedom seemed to draw them toward the access road like a giant magnet. They were too excited to speak.

"We've forgotten Candy!" said Irene, breaking the silence.

The group stopped guiltily. Their eyes turned to the crumpled body.

"We can't leave her there," Irene said.

They wanted to continue their flight, yet no one could say that Candy should be left unattended. Each one looked to the other for a decision.

"You guys go on to the sheriff's car," Big Jim said. "The long drink and me'll get Candy and put her in the refrigerator. We'll meet you out on the road. Wait for us. Okay?"

"Do it," Whitney said. "Don't be gone too long."

"Don't worry about it. Ain't nobody wants to get out of this place quicker'n me," said Long John.

"I want to help," said Katie suddenly.

"What for? We can handle it," said Big Jim.

"Because I was her friend, that's what for."

Katie had her eyes fixed on Irene. Her volunteering seemed an act of bravado, as though here, at the last minute, she could prove herself as strong as Irene.

"Sure, kid," said Big Jim. "Tell you what, you go back of the garage and get one of those big plastic bags. We'll get a sheet."

Big Jim, Long John, and Katie went about their tasks, while the others went to the car.

"Boy, she's got some kind of bug," said Long John.

"Yeah."

"I can't see nobody doing a thing like this unless they have to."

"Like you say," said Big Jim, "she's got a bug."

"I been noticing you and Irene, man. You hung up on her?" asked Big Jim, not looking up.

"I don't know. She's a hell of a broad."

"Nice, though," said Big Jim.

His friend was silent for a couple of seconds, lost in thought. "Yeah."

They walked away silently. Long John, with his towering height, and Big Jim, massive and compact, seemed equal ends of an equation, flip sides of the same coin.

Long John looked over his shoulder and saw the

remainder of their group disappear into the eucalytpus grove. The two men were alone again. Long John smiled to think of that. It was so natural. That's the way it had been for a long time: just the two of them, but more like one person.

At their first meeting in high school they had one hell of fight. Always had to prove yourself, Long John thought. Jim had finally cut him down with fists like hammers.

Whatever point that was supposed to make, was made, and they had been hanging around together ever since. Couple of years in the merchant marines, a tour in Nam, construction jobs ever since.

Suddenly, Katie screamed, but it was cut off almost as soon as it began.

Big Jim and Long John dashed toward the sound. As they swung around the corner of the house, a rifle, swung by the muzzle, smashed into Long John's belly. He doubled over and crashed backward. In the same instant, a stick of firewood, wielded like a club, grazed the side of Big Jim's head. He spun crazily, clutching at the pain. The club struck again, this time across the back of the neck. Like a felled tree, Big Jim toppled.

Neither Big Jim nor Long John saw Katie, thrashing like a captured butterfly, her mouth stuffed with a grimy handkerchief, being hauled away by two bikers.

"What was that?" said the sheriff as he held the car door open. "Sounded like a scream. Maybe it was that girl."

"Katie," Irene supplied.

"Yeah. I wonder if they're having any trouble back there."

"What kind of trouble could they be having?" Pat asked. "Long John and Big Jim seem quite capable of handling any trouble that comes along. Katie responds— uh—rather emotionally to certain situations."

"You mean the same way the rest of us do?" Irene asked icily.

"I didn't mean . . ." Pat began defensively, but was cut off by the sheriff.

"I guess everything's all right," he said.

The moment the sheriff turned the key in his own car, he heard the ignition of the convertible on the other side of the grove roar to life. "Guess it was nothing. They're in the Caddy now," he said. "Good."

Slowly coaxing the accelerator, Whitney eased the police car across the customers' parking lot, waiting for the other to catch up.

"God, I can hardly wait to get out of here," Pat said.

Costaign looked back at her and smiled. "Me, too," he grinned. Even as he smiled, Costaign felt he had somehow missed an opportunity with her. Since he met her yesterday morning, he had the feeling that she would be somehow involved in his new life.

"Here they come now," said Irene, anxiously turning around in her seat and watching the car zoom up from behind the trees. "Hey," she said, "that's not . . ."

"Sheriff! Look out!" Pat screamed.

The Cadillac, occupied by four intense bikers instead of the three friends they expected, raced up to the police car. A burst of gunfire spurted from the Caddy, but the sheriff instinctively jerked the wheel to the right. A shower of slugs, intended for the driver's door, splattered into the left rear fender and trunk.

The police car rocked dizzily as it tried to recover from the sharp veer. Pat and Irene screamed. Costaign slid to the floor.

"Je-sus Christ!" Whitney crouched his head over the wheel as he fought the momentum.

The Caddy did not pursue. It raced to the access road, where it pulled across, blocking the way. The occupants hunkered down as though in a trench, prepared to resist an attack.

The sheriff's car straightened out, and another blast of gunfire whistled over the roof. Whitney spun the car into a long elliptical curve and aimed it right back toward the house. Another volley whizzed overhead.

In a minute, Pat, Irene, Costaign were pouring from the car and scrambling across the porch.

"Get inside," Whitney yelled. "I'm going to get on the radio."

He clicked impatiently at the "On" switch. Nothing happened. The red eye continued to stare blindly. Holding the microphone in his hand, he realized the coiled wire connecting the mike to the radio had been cut.

"Sonofabitch!"

The sheriff stared angrily at the wire until the scream of the convertible's engine, as it rocked around the edge of the grove, galvanized him. Swinging the door open, in a single motion he dove for the porch and crashed through the door, his Magnum in hand.

The Caddy quivered to a halt in front of the porch.

There was a moment of tenseness as the bikers decided what to do next. The sheriff made their decision for them. From his kneeling position, he boomed off one shot. It split the air beside Banzo's ear. The Caddy jackrabbited to life. It dug its way in a tight circle around the lawn, coming to rest directly in front of the eucalyptus grove. The four bikers slid out behind it.

Alert and poised, the sheriff could hear scurrying among the trees. Footsteps seemed to fan out in all directions. Whitney tried to follow the direction of the sounds above the pounding in his own ears.

Costaign crawled across the floor of the parlor and joined the sheriff. The women crouched behind the divans.

"Keep your head down, Doc. They ain't finished shooting yet."

"What can I do to help? Have you got another gun?"

"There was a shotgun out in the car, but if them guys were sneaky enough to cut the radio wire while we were talking a while ago, sure as hell they've got it. This is a hell of a thing. No radio. Phone wires cut. And they got all the guns."

Costaign lay flat, not asking the sheriff how he knew the phone wires had been cut. Everyone was silent as the seconds ticked.

"Hey, Sheriff!!" Banzo's voice called. "You hear me

you lying rat? Come on out. We want to rap with you."

Costaign looked up and saw the sheriff as stony featured and steady as a statue. He wondered what he himself looked like. All he knew was that the inside of his belly was clenched and his thighs were tingling. He hoped his fear didn't show on his face.

"Come on, man! You're in there. Don't pull no silent treatment on us. We want to talk to you. We don't want to waste nobody. We could have done it a few minutes ago, but we shot over your heads."

"Sure you did, you bastard," the sheriff muttered to himself.

"What are you going to do? You're not going out there?" Costaign asked.

"That would be suicide," Pat said from across the room.

Costaign threw a sharp glance at her. He realized in that silly moment, even as he felt the anger, that he wanted her to remain in the background and accept what was going on in the doorway as *men's* work.

"You bet your tail I ain't walking," said the sheriff. "I'm going to tag them right, but I ain't walking into nothing."

"What happened to Long John—and Big Jim?" Irene asked.

"That's right," Pat added, "and Katie?"

"I don't know. They're out there someplace. We'll be hearing from them," Whitney said.

"Okay, wise ass. You fucked us over, now you ain't got the guts to face the shit. You will, man. You can play all the games you want, but you're gonna face it. Man, what'ya think, we're dumb?" Banzo's voice again.

Only silence answered him.

"Dig this, then," Banzo continued. "You only got the daylight. Maybe another eight hours. Understand? Then them roaches will be coming back. How does that grab you, huh? And you ain't going nowhere either. We got that pad surrounded. First one sticks his head out the door gets blown away. Unless it's you with your hands up. You gave me the gun, Sheriff, and Uncle Sam taught me to use it. Ain't that a bitch? So you think about it. You hear me? *You face us or you face them fucking roaches!* Eight hours you got. We'll be here when you make up your mind."

Fear filled the room like a breath of frost at the mention of the roaches. The sheriff's resolve nearly collapsed when he thought of how he'd dragged these innocent people into such horror: first by accident; now, to save his own miserable skin. He looked into Costaign's face to see if an accusation were there. There was nothing.

"These people ain't done nothing to you!" Whitney called out. "You let them go. I'll come out hands up."

"Sheriff! . . ." Pat began, like a reproving school teacher.

"Fuck you!" Banzo shouted. "They ain't no skin off my ass one way or the other. We want *you*. You reminded me. Don't be looking for them two big dudes to save you, hear? They're gonzo. Forget it. And you know that little blond slit? Well, she's keeping us company. In case you have trouble making up your mind to come out, in a couple of minutes she's going to start hollering. Longer you stay in there, the louder she's going to holler. You got it? Give you what they call 'an incentive.' Dig? It's an old Indian thing, man. I saw it in a flick."

"They've got Katie!" Costaign whispered in despair.

"Oh my God," said Irene. "And what happened to Long John!"

"That's it," the sheriff said, "I'll go out. Those bastards ain't kidding. They'll torture Katie. I can't have you people suffering for my mistakes."

"Maybe that biker is right, Sheriff. Maybe you are an asshole," said Irene brutally.

Whitney looked around, stunned.

"Don't be a fool. You know that type out there. I know them, too. More than you think. You're not going to help anybody by going out there and giving them what they want." Irene was mad. She drew a deep breath and continued.

"Sorry, Sheriff—I was just trying to get your attention. I appreciate what you're trying to do, but I thought you knew better. You walk out there and they'll kill you. With you out of the way, that leaves Dr. Costaign, Dr. Symington, and me, alone. With those guns, you know what they'll do to Dr. Costaign. And I don't have to tell you what they'll do to Dr. Symington and me. In the end, they're not going to let anyone out alive."

Costaign burned under Irene's implication that he

couldn't protect the women. He burned mainly because he knew it was true.

"They wouldn't dare!" said Pat with sudden indignation.

"Don't kid yourself. Ask the sheriff. He knows," Irene said.

"You got all the answers. What do we do?" Whitney asked, glad to have the burden of decision on this matter taken from him.

"I say we sit tight. We don't know what happened to Long John or Big Jim or Katie. Lots of things can happen in eight hours. Let's just keep our cool."

"I say you're right. What about you others? You agree with her? It's your lives we're talking about," Whitney said.

"I think Irene is right," said Costaign. "It wouldn't help us a bit if you went out. I'm not much of a fighter. And if I have to do any fighting I'd rather have you with me than be alone."

The sheriff looked to Pat. Terror shining on her face, she nodded agreement.

Anton Whitney looked at them gratefully. He lifted his right hand and sighted along the barrel of the Magnum. Another round roared out across the lawn and splattered in the trees.

It was immediately followed by a volley of automatic fire that slivered the window next to the sheriff.

"Okay!" Banzo called. "You want it. You got it. Remember: eight hours." Then the voice added ominously, "If you don't care what happens to blondie."

The sheriff looked at the watch around his wrist as though it were a bomb. Eight hours.

At first everything was red along the edges. Then the red poured inward across the darkness, like paint dripping down an easel. Long John opened his eyes. The red gradually faded. After a few moments of swirling, things took their normal positions in recognizable objects. A streak of white hot pain stitched its way across his belly, and he remembered everything. He carefully felt around with his hands. He felt no open wounds.

It didn't seem as though anything were broken either. Each minute, more life poured into him.

His eyes fell upon Big Jim, lying about two yards from him.

"Hey, Jimbo." Long John's voice was hoarse. "Hey, you big sonofabitch. You all right?"

No answer. Long John dug his fingers into the earth. Slowly—the pain in his solar plexus searing him—he dragged himself until he could reach his friend. "Hey," he gasped, touching the inert body. "Hey." He shook Big Jim gently. "You all right? Hey, Jimbo."

Long John's effort was, at last, rewarded by a groan.

"That's it, you sonofabitch. Wake up. Where're you hit?"

Big Jim's hands clamped his head. He groaned deeply and rolled over. Long John saw that the right side of Big Jim's head was discolored, his eye swollen shut, as distended and shiny as a melon.

"Bastards," Long John hissed. He continued unsuccessfully to rouse his friend. The roar of the sheriff's Magnum, in the distance, did what Long John couldn't.

One eye in big Jim's twisted face opened. ". . . the hell was that?" The eye, after several attempts at focusing, settled on Long John. "Jesus, I remember. What hit me? Oh, my goddam head."

"You okay?"

"Yeah. I think so."

"That sure as hell was a shot. Something big, too."

They heard men's voices shouting, but they could make no sense of it. Together they crawled on their bellies to a watering spigot on the side of the hacienda. Long John held Big Jim's head under the cool water.

A spurt of automatic weapon fire shattered the calm.

"Let's get some cover till we find out what's going on," said Big Jim. He spotted a tree nearby, and both men started to crawl toward it. At one spot where Big Jim planted his hand for support, the ground fell away into a deep hole. He withdrew his arm quickly, but did not move. "Hey, look at this."

The undermined earth he had dislodged seemed to be the beginning of a chain reaction. In several places, beneath the house, out on the path, in the grass, little swirling holes magically appeared. The entire area seemed to be slowly caving in on itself.

Both men, moving gingerly ducked around back to the entrance of the garage. Just as they approached the door, a barrage of bullets splashed into the door.

When the weight finally lifted itself from her, Katie

closed her legs and rolled over. Next to her, on the ground, were the tattered remains of what had been the paisley pajamas she had put on so short a time ago. The shaggy man standing at her feet was sweaty and odorous as he pulled his pants back up. Katie's eyes were wet with unshed tears of rage. This bastard, and the one before him, had just robbed her. She struggled to find words for what they had done, but found only inchoate, scalding rage.

Rape. She had never imagined it. After all, she knew what she was. She had always thought of it as something that happened to other women. She had also thought that the women made too much of it. Now she knew that everything they had said was true. Every last dumb word. It had nothing to do with sex, and she was a girl who knew a little about sex. It was an arrogant brutal insult. She now felt the killing anger she had only read about before.

Oh, no, she thought as three more bikers joined the one who had just finished with her. She closed her ears to their lascivious comments. In doing so, she missed other things they chuckled about.

She was startled when they dragged her to her feet. "Hey," she said as they pushed and shoved her to a spot a little deeper into the grove. "Why don't you apes take it easy. I ain't got no shoes on."

The four laughed at her nakedness.

In a clearing, her hands were untied. She was again thrown to the ground. One of the bikers produced more rope from his pocket.

"What are you guys doing? What do you need

all the ropes for? Take it easy! Hey, that hurts!"

Four widespread pegs had been driven into the ground to make a square. In an instant, each man, taking a foot or a hand, had her spread-eagled on her back, binding her hands and feet to the pegs.

"This is crazy," Katie screamed. "What are you doing?"

She struggled futilely. Once she was secured, one of the bikers called out toward the Caddy, barely visible on the fringe of the trees. "Do it," a voice screamed in return.

The grinning bikers knelt around Katie. Her wide, frightened eyes jumped from one to the other. "What do you want? What are you going to do?" One of the men removed a Zippo lighter from his jacket pocket. He struck a flame. "What are you going to do with that!" Katie was terrified now. Lightly he touched the flame to her armpit. "Hey. Hey! What are you doing? Don't! DON'T!!"

Katie's scream was long and shrill.

Irene was alone in the kitchen when she heard it. She pressed her head against the wall. Oh God. They're doing it. She suddenly regretted her conversation with Whitney. She had no idea what it would be like to have Katie's screams prod her like a barb.

There was a pause after the scream died away. Tears trickled down Irene's cheeks. "No. No. No," she said aloud as the scream resumed. "Oh, leave her alone!" Irene pressed her palms against her ears.

"What the hell is that?" said a gruff voice behind her.

Standing in the doorway from the garage was Long John supporting Big Jim with his left shoulder. The woman ran to him, but stopped when she saw Big Jim's face.

"Who's doing the screaming?" Big Jim asked.

Realizing Big Jim was all right, at least all right enough to talk, Irene pressed herself against Long John's chest.

"It's Katie. The bikers are torturing her, to get the sheriff to come out so they can kill him."

"Bikers? A motorcycle gang. Them the guys that had the guns yesterday? The same bastards that hit us?"

Irene explained what she could as she accompanied the two men into the parlor. The sheriff, Costaign, and Pat greeted the two men unrestrainedly. Even so, the faces of those in the parlor were tense, their bodies, too, as though they would leap at a touch. Their nervous systems seemed connected to the cycles of Katie's shrieks.

Costaign and the sheriff continued filling in Long John and Big Jim in their situation with Banzo. All the while Katie's screams raked their spines. Finally, Pat cracked. "Why don't they stop! I can't stand this!" Costaign quickly grasped her shoulder. "Get your medical bag," he said softly. "Take care of Big Jim." The sudden reminder of duty galvanized her. Costaign remembered that she had been like this once before and noted the characteristic. "We'll take care of that scene in a little while," Big Jim said to Pat as she went to get her medical bag.

Looking to the others, Big Jim said, "I think we got

another problem. Maybe a big one. All them goddam roaches are burrowing. They've got this gulley undermined, and I don't know how bad. I know they're doing a job on the outside of the house near the vegetable locker, where we just were. I don't know what this house uses for a foundation, for all we know it could be air by now. We may not even have eight hours."

CHAPTER
TWELVE

Sergeant Gomez pointed his car up the mountain, oblivious to the expanses that moved past him, and to the way they narrowed down to rocky cliffs allowing him only quick glimpses of view. His mind was struggling with the problem of Eros Ranch. Though it had seemed like a good idea when he told Deigan he would check on the boss, now he was assaulted by doubts. He was feeling vaguely disloyal to the man to whom he owed so much.

He did not go home after work. He called his wife from Harry's, where he had been sloshing up a couple of beers.

"Christ, Emil, I'm not used to seeing you here at this

hour," Harry had said. "All you guys from the sheriff's department are acting flaky lately."

No wonder, Gomez thought. After spending most of the morning drinking beer, he finally decided. What can it hurt if I just check with him? Who knows, maybe he could use a little help. Maybe the sheriff was in trouble. On the other hand, the sheriff might have something going he didn't want *anybody* in on. Maybe I'll go crashing in and screw everything up, he thought.

Gomez considered the dead telephone line, the lack of radio communication. A lot of nutty things had been happening. The whole business was crazy right from the start.

He was still in turmoil as he braked for the roadblock, where he stepped out to join two khaki-uniformed patrolmen.

"Checking up, huh, Gomez?"

"Damn right. You guys can't be trusted to do nothing," he joked.

"You just finished up at eight this morning, didn't you? How come you ain't home?" one of the cops asked.

" 'Cause I can't stand to be away from you guys."

Both cops laughed. "There's a sick man."

Gomez lifted his face to the sun. "So this is what fresh air smells like," he said, inhaling noisily. He noted the supple treetops bending under the pressure of the wind, up above the flanking hills.

For all his light talk, Gomez was driven by an inner urge to get to Eros Ranch. The wind, with its sound of rushing, added impetus to his feeling.

"You guys hear anything from Eros?" he asked.

"Like what?"

"Like anything."

"Nope."

"Nothing that sounds like trouble?" Gomez persisted. "No word from the boss? Nothing out of the ordinary?"

"What could we hear?" asked one of the cops, perplexed at Gomez's insistence.

"Nothing's good to hear, I guess," said Gomez.

"You going up to have a look around?"

Gomez was torn from a long minute. "Naw," he said, at last. "If you guys didn't hear nothing, I guess I'll save myself the trip. Think I'll go home and pound the pillow."

"Or whoever's available, huh? Don't kid me, I used to be on nights," one of the cops grinned.

Her body was like a machine out of control. It twisted and writhed of its own volition, while her mind, in order to save itself, withdrew into a tiny corner of her head. Pain by pain, the bikers had taken her body over. With each new application of the flame, they seemed to plant another independent control within her naked flesh. Each separate spot of fiery agony required its own response: on the soles of her blistered bare feet, on her inner thighs, in her armpits.

"Not there, man," one of the bikers had laughed in answer to an obscene suggestion, "we're saving that."

Katie's throat was raw. Her wrists and ankles were bloody from their struggles with the ropes. She no longer felt human. She was no more than a captive animal that made mindless noises whenever the bikers wanted them.

She was finally allowed a respite from the torture when Banzo stepped into the clearing. Oh, thank God, she thought.

"Now that ain't a very ladylike position," he taunted her, while the others laughed. "Give it a break for a while. We've given them something to think about for the last hour."

The bikers sat back from Katie, disappointed, then slowly stood up. Katie sobbed in gratitude.

"Don't think you're beating city hall, there, gorgeous. That pig friend of yours doesn't come through, you're going to be singing again. Real soon."

"Almost noon," the sheriff said.

Their strategy meeting was brief and uncomplicated. They knew precisely how much time they had. Banzo shouted from the trees that he was going to give Katie a half hour rest while they made up their minds to send the sheriff out.

"Screw them guys," said Big Jim, "we'll sift their ashes in a hurry." Pat was just finishing up treating his wound. "The real problem," he continued, "is the roaches. We got to find a way to get Katie and split this place all at the same time. 'Cause we ain't got too much time."

Big Jim had stated the problem succinctly: the roaches. Live or die. The roaches or the guns.

"How much artillery we got, Sheriff?" Long John asked.

"Just this." He hefted the Magnum.

"Nothing in the car?"

The sheriff explained that the bikers had probably stolen his shotgun.

"Shit. Wouldn't the security guards have left some sort of weapons here in the house?" said Long John.

"Not a chance," said Irene. "These places are so strictly supervised by the state even the guards have to have special licenses. If there *are* any guns around, I've never heard of them. Management didn't like the idea either: having guns where some hostile drunk might find them."

"Then we got one," said Big Jim. "And it ain't shit up against a couple of M-16s. But it's all we got."

"What the hell are you talking about?" the sheriff asked. "We can't get into no fire fight, even if we had the guns. We got innocent people around here."

"Well," Long John said, "that means we got to use our brains. How many of these guys are there? All told?"

"Seven," the sheriff answered.

"Right. That's seven armed men."

Everyone was silent as they considered Long Jim's words.

"That creep Banzo says they got the house surrounded. The guys with Katie have got the front of the house covered, so where would you put the other four to cover the rest of it?" Big Jim asked.

"Figure they must be pretty smart. From what the sheriff says about them cutting the phone lines and the radio looks like they got this thing planned out," Long John said.

"Right. That Banzo has got his men in the right places—where they would each have the best field of fire," Whitney added.

Big Jim was staring at his feet as he began, "Only two people know the terrain that well: you and Irene." He gazed at the woman.

"Count me out," Irene piped in. "I'm strictly an indoors type. That leaves the sheriff."

It was apparent that Whitney's mind was already working before Irene passed the buck.

"You know, goddamit, Big Jim," the sheriff said thoughtfully, "you're right. How come I never thought of that? I not only know this area better than anybody in this room, I know it better than *them*."

"Now you're talking," said Big Jim.

"Let's take it step by step. We know the front of the house is covered and we know where they are. What about the back?"

"It's one mammy of a steep cliff. You couldn't put a gun right on top because the house is right up against the cliff. The only thing you could see would be the roof," said Long John.

"When we was outside," said Big Jim, "just as we were coming in, some guy squeezed off a burst. It seemed to come from the side, beyond the spud locker."

"That figures," said the sheriff. "They couldn't put it no place else."

"That's right," Long John crowed. "You got it, Sheriff. They'd put two guys up against the cliff in the back and to the side so they could see down that little space between the house and the cliff."

"And that's enough to cover us," Big Jim growled. "Three in front, two in the back, and two on the sides. Christ, what a trap this place is. One way out and there are three guys with AWs between us and it."

"Maybe it ain't as bad as all that," said Whitney. "You got me thinking about the country hereabouts. This gulley we're in ain't exactly a hole in the ground. Used to be part of a spillway for Lake Campbell. You know, it would rain and the lake would overflow. I hear they used to have the goddamdest flash floods. That's why the walls are so steep. They built kind of a dam a couple of years ago to keep the lake from spilling over this way.

"Seems to me we don't have to go out the front way. If we can get over to the hill on the right side of the house, we might be able to find the waterway and scoot on up the hill."

"You mean," Big Jim said, "there's a gulley that runs all the way up this mountain?"

"Well, I ain't really seen it. But I read about it in the county hall of records. I'm a guy who likes to keep his eye on things, you know? If nobody else knows about it, maybe it's because it's been shut off for some years now."

"I remember hearing people talk down at the Sunburst Hotel that they couldn't run a road from Cherakowa to Lake Campbell until they found some way to deal with the flash floods they used to have," said Costaign.

"God damn," said Big Jim, grinning.

"That's our out," said Long John.

Their grins spread to the others.

"Now we have to think of some way to get Katie," said Irene.

"That's next on the agenda," said Long John. "And it's going to be a bitch."

"Hey, long drink," said Big Jim, "why don't you check out the right side of the house? See if you can spot where they got their men, and see if you can see that spillway? While you're doing that, I'll do the left side."

"Okay with me. You feeling up to it?"

Big Jim touched his swollen face. "Hurts like a bastard, but I'm okay. Hey, Doc, you want to come along? I got something to show you."

Costaign almost answered before he realized Big Jim was talking to Pat.

"All right," she answered.

"Why don't *I* go with you. It's too dangerous! I don't like the idea of Pat—I mean, Dr. Symington—risking her life," said Costaign.

Pat shot a withering look, then turned to Big Jim. "Let's get started," she said. "You just show me what you want me to do."

"Look, here . . ." Costaign began.

"I thought Doc Symington was the big authority on insects," said Big Jim.

"Well—she is."

"That's what I need: an authority on insects. And that ain't you," said Big Jim.

Pat glowed triumphantly as she and Big Jim exited. Costaign stood smoldering. But for three people's exquisite self-control, he would have been surrounded by smiles.

"Don't worry," said Irene, with innocent composure, "she won't get—hurt."

Their mood was broken by Banzo's voice booming from the trees. "Better hurry up, Sheriff. You got fifteen minutes left."

CHAPTER
THIRTEEN

The sweat of fear and pain that glistened on Katie's body had begun to evaporate when she heard Banzo call to the house. His fifteen minute warning made her shudder. "No. For God's sake. Please," she whispered aloud through cracked lips. Her wounds, which had eased during her respite, began throbbing again. Unconsciously, she tugged at the pegs that held her.

She was alone in the tiny clearing. Her four tormentors had gone to join Banzo at the convertible. She was grateful to be free of their salacious comments, if only for a few minutes. Pulling at her bonds was already a reflex. She suddenly felt an electric shock when she realized the peg holding her right wrist was loosening.

She looked in disbelief along the length of her arm. She jerked the wrist experimentally and watched the stake wobble. She noted that the soil holding it seemed to be receding around the base.

She stopped. How soon would they be back? Did she have time—? Suddenly her thoughts didn't matter. The prospect of renewed torture prodded her like a hot spear. She gasped as she concentrated all her strength into her right arm. It was almost impossible to exert leverage, tied as she was, but she pulled and jerked and tugged. The sweat began again. This time it was the sweat of frantic physical labor.

"Just take it easy," Big Jim said. "There's a dude out there with an M-16 trained on this door. I'm going to throw this garbage can out, up high. As soon as you hear the fire, we'll scoot out way down low on our bellies. Okay? We'll make it right around the corner and head for the vegetable locker. Know which one I mean? Once we clear the corner we'll be safe."

Pat nodded.

"Scared?" Big Jim asked.

Again Pat nodded affirmatively.

"Me, too," he smiled. "Don't worry too much. They don't want to waste us, they're after Whitney. Just be cool, and move fast."

Pat looked down at herself. "Do you think these clothes'll take it," she asked.

"Doc, you're okay." The big man smiled.

The garbage can clanged into three others standing along the base of the cliff. At the same time Pat and

Big Jim, looking like two furious crabs, scuttled around the corner. A stream of gunfire rained onto the row of cans, then stitched across the ground they had just vacated. The pair flattened themselves under the wooden vegetable locker.

"Hey, Banzo!" a voice called. "Two of them just ducked out to that little wooden building by the garage. I can't get them from here!"

Pat's and Big Jim's blood turned to frost as they saw a young man, his M-16 held at high port, zigzag out from behind the convertible. They were helpless! If they stayed he would get them; if they tried to make it back, the snipers would.

One shot boomed out from the hacienda doorway. The runner was smashed backward as though he'd been hit by a baseball bat. He didn't even flop around when he hit the ground.

Another volley from the woods chewed the porch and the doorjamb, but it was too late. The bikers had blown it with a dumb recruit mistake. They had let a man expose himself without cover. And the sheriff was obviously not the guy to make that mistake with.

"Good ol' Whitney," said Big Jim.

Pat was too terrified to speak.

"I know how you feel," he said, touching her arm. "They won't send anybody else. We're okay. They just found out what the sheriff can do with that pistol. Come over here with me. This is what I want to show you."

On their bellies they slithered to a spot from which they could see the eroding base of the house. The holes had gotten immense since the last time Big Jim had seen them, and there were more of them.

"Look," said Pat as she eyed the holes, the ground, and the brick bases of the hacienda. They were alive with roaches, dozens of nits for every adult, and empty sacs everywhere.

"They're multiplying like crazy," she continued in disbelief.

"That's what I wanted to show you. Man, in one day, there must be three or four times the roaches we had last night. What's making them reproduce like that?"

Pat's expression changed. She was no longer the scared woman in a world of violence, she was again the scientist in her lab. She studied the roaches, which swarmed like ants on a hill, as though by looking she could determine the mechanics of their genes.

"I've been thinking about it," she said. "And I can't make any sense out of it. Not only what's making them reproduce, but what made them congregate at Eros Ranch. Whatever increased their reproductive cycle is happening to them right here in the gulley. The real question is, How long will they stay in the gulley? There's food here. Maybe that's what's keeping them. There's no substance on earth that a roach won't eat, including its own discarded skin. By that definition, there should be food enough here to last them for a while. But at the rate they're reproducing, how long will it be before they spread out into nearby towns? I think that's the question.

"If it weren't for these insane motorcyclists, we could have health department extermination crews up here already. By the time we get some sort of terms worked out with the bikers, or until we escape, it may be too late. The roaches may be spread all over the countryside by then."

Before the doctor's observations could be carried any further, a sudden ruckus erupted from the woods behind the convertible. Shouts and bellowing confusion filled the air. Without warning, Katie, racing like a hunted fox, dashed from the trees. Her legs pumped like pistons. Her hair flew out behind her. Another biker dashed out behind her. Only an arm's length away!

Another shot streaked from the doorway, and the pursuing biker spun like a toy!

"Here! Katie, over here! The vegetable locker! It's me, Big Jim! Get over here, quick!"

Just as the frightened woman cleared the corner of the house a shower of bullets ripped it to flying splinters. Pat and Big Jim dragged Katie to safety under the floorboards. Both flinched when they saw her blistered sides and legs.

At least the bikers had lost another man. Now there were five. That sheriff was a mother with his elephant gun! Big Jim began his tactical mathematics again. Two dead. That left five. He began to wonder if their original analysis of the bikers' positioning had been correct. Judging from the amount of gunfire coming from behind the Caddy, there must have been more than three guys there. Even with two dead, they were still able to send up quite a volley. Maybe there weren't two guys guarding each side of the house. Maybe there was only one. He began to wonder if they may have overestimated Banzo's brains.

Big Jim knew they had to get back into the house now. That was going to be a bitch because that one guy knew where they were and sure as hell he'd be keeping his eye on the garage door. How were they going to get in?

A sudden movement off on the periphery of his vision gave him his answer.

He gently pushed both women.

"Go!" he said. "Run! In the garage door!"

"What the fucking hell are you doing here!"

Banzo was in a rage. Boris, the biker who had fired on Big Jim and Pat, had fled down to the Caddy. While he ran he knew just what he was gong to tell Banzo. Now confronting the leader, Boris was hypnotized by Banzo's bulging red-streaked eyes, the veins standing out on his forehead, pulsing like angry worms.

"Jesus Christ! That goddam sheriff could be making it out the back door! What'r'ya, out of your skull? Get back there right now before I blow your frigging dumb ass away!"

Boris found his tongue. "You nuts or something? Bullshit. You want us all to get wasted? Look at them two, man." Boris gestured in the direction of his fallen friends. "I ain't getting my ass blown away. Screw offing that sheriff. This whole idea is crazy. I'm getting out. I'm splitting right now!"

"Carmine!" Banzo shouted to the biker crouched

behind the car. "Get over on that hill behind the house. Quick. Replace this chicken-shit sonofabitch."

Carmine, still stunned by the gunning of his two friends because death came so suddenly, followed Banzo's orders, but he did so heavily and without conviction.

"Come on, Banz," Boris pleaded, "let's all split while we still can. It's crazy, what we're doing, and you know it."

"Every cop in Nevada is looking for us now. We need that sheriff to get us out of here," Banzo said.

"Not me," said Boris. "I'd rather get busted. I don't need no fucking bullet in my head." He was feeling bolder.

"After us shooting at a cop and fucking around with that slit, you think all you're going to get is good time? Forget it. Judges got dirty names for them things. You take a shot at a cop and you're lucky if you ever get to court."

"Not me. I'm out. You can have this one." Boris threw the M-16 to the ground. He turned and strode away from Banzo, through the trees.

Banzo snapped his rifle up to this shoulder, aiming it at the center of Boris's back. Then he lowered it. "No," he said aloud, "payback is a motherfucker."

He hadn't realized that Cutter, the only one remaining with him, had been watching.

"Let's do what we came here to do. Screw Boris," said Cutter.

"Payback is a motherfucker," Banzo again said

softly. Cutter noticed that something was missing from Banzo's face. He now had the expression of one who stares too hard into the sun.

As Boris cleared the woods, he breathed an audible sigh of relief. He had been sure Banzo was going to give it to him in the back. Once clear, he ran. He figured to get about halfway down the access road, then cut up through the woods, take off for Vegas. Soon he was breathing heavily from the thin mountain air.

Then there was no air. About thirty feet from the beginning of the road, the earth opened and swallowed Boris in one big gulp. He didn't have time to scream as he dropped into the cauldron teeming with cockroaches . . . and was immediately engulfed! For a few hysterical moments, he thrashed. Soon he was merely a lump beneath the black, tarlike surface.

Crouched around the right wheel of the Caddy, Banzo scanned the front of the hacienda along the barrel of his rifle. No. The sheriff hadn't gone. Even as he thought this, he wondered how things had suddenly turned around. An hour ago, the world had been his oyster. His little force was now down to four.

As he stared at the hacienda, his eyes seemed to waver. A tiny pinpoint of vacuum seemed to grow in his head.

Pat took Katie to one of the upstairs rooms to clean and dress her wounds and found herself admiring Katie for enduring the process with clenched teeth. Not so much for her strength in enduring the physical pain of having her wounds cleaned—the bikers had not

een kind to her—but in her sense of knowing her own
ealities. Katie was an earthy person who understood
hings physical. She was scared, of course, but not with
mindless panic. She was angry. At least she understood
what had happened: men and sex, two subjects with
which she was very familiar.

Looking at Katie, and realizing that she only feared
hose things she didn't understand, Pat saw through a
dark mirror into herself. Was it the same with her? In
a strange way, these hours at Eros were her first real
contact with an uncontrived reality. She had learned
hings about herself that she hadn't been able to sort
nto neat boxes. Some had even shamed her. In her
eyes she had come off second best to people she considered culturally inferior to herself. Lucky Katie, Pat
mused, to be able to go through life unbothered by such
stupid things.

"That's it," Pat said, "you're as pretty as a picture
again."

Downstairs, the sheriff was still crouched behind the
doorjamb. He viewed the two corpses sprawled on the
lawn. He looked intensely then at the car. One good
shot, that's all I need.

Long John handed Katie a stiff bourbon. "Here, you
earned this. How you feeling?"

"Okay," the woman answered.

"You, too," he said, handing a drink to Pat.

"You're quite a lady, Doc," said Big Jim from across
the room. "In case medicine ever goes to hell, you're
going to make a good living in Spesh Force."

Long John laughed aloud. "Chee-rist, I haven't

heard that in a long time." To Irene and Pat: "The big guy and me once did a hitch training Cambodian Rangers, and that's what they called us—U.S. Special Forces. When they said it it sounded like *Use Spesh Force.* I think he's complimenting you there, Doc."

"We never had any of them fancy outfits when I was a kid, in Korea," said the sheriff, never taking his eyes off the Caddy. "We was just plain old dogface soldiers."

"You also didn't have Walter Cronkite following you around either. We were just the same thing, but we had to have all them fancy names to make the people back home think we were somebody," said Big Jim.

"Where were you in Korea?" asked Long John.

"Pusan Perimeter. 1950."

"You sure learned how to use that popgun. That was some of the nicest shooting I've ever seen," said Big Jim.

The sheriff beamed under the compliment. "Thanks," he said. "What about outside? Did you locate their people?"

Big Jim explained his feelings. "So, things may be better than we think. I don't believe they got two guys on each side. I believe they got one. Maybe ol' Banzo ain't as smart as we give him credit for."

"He's plenty smart. If he's doing dumb things, I don't know why."

"Let's make sure. Hey, tall boy, how'd you like to go upstairs on the second floor and get a room facing the right-hand hill out there, the one with the waterway? See if you can pinpoint their boy? I'll do the same over on the left."

"Okay with me," said Long John. "I wonder why they didn't spread their people out more?"

"Maybe they're scared. Scared people tend to cluster," said Costaign.

"You know, Doc, you may be right. And that's something to think about," said Whitney. "Maybe they're more afraid of us than we are of them."

"Yeah," said Big Jim. "After all, Whitney here is a sheriff, and it's usually a heavy thing to gun a sheriff. Shooting cops is bad business. And when they lost Katie, they lost the only real weapon they had."

In a brief conference, they decided to wait out the afternoon.

"Sure," Big Jim had said. "Let's test *their* nerve. If they were here last night, they know what them roaches looked like, and they ain't no more eager to meet them again than we are. We'll wait right down to the last minute. See if they crack."

If the bikers' nerve held, they would rush the one man holding the right-hand hill and make it to the spillway.

Even though things seemed to be moving their way for a change, there was much bravado but little joy. It still promised to be a long afternoon, surrounded by the dead, and those who might soon be dead.

The sun of early afternoon cut thin shadows onto the floor of the upstairs room. Long John knelt, as unmoving as a Cherokee Indian, behind one of the window curtains. He surveyed the area in the direction of the brush-covered spillway, looking for a single, telltale motion. There had been no shouts from the bikers outside for over an hour, and no visible activity. From all appearances they might be gone. He knew they weren't.

Perhaps they, too, had fallen into the laziness of afternoon. Long John felt it strongly. The impasse, now that Katie was back, had given them all a chance to relax. Funny the things that float up to the surface of your mind, even if it is only a simple thing like getting drowsy in the afternoon. Before he had come upstairs, Katie had put together a lunch of bits and pieces from the small refrigerator behind the bar. It occurred to him he hadn't eaten in close to forty-eight hours as he wolfed the cold cocktail sausages, cheese hors d'oeuvres, olives, pearl onions, and pretzels.

The seven occupants of the house, perhaps all under the spell of afternoon, had drifted away from one another as though each wanted to sort through the closets of his head. All except the sheriff, of course. He never moved a muscle from the door.

Hours were going by. Half their allotted eight were gone already. They were playing a dangerous game with the bikers, waiting until the last minute like this. If it didn't work. . . .

"Hi."

Long John turned to see Irene standing beside the door.

"Hi yourself."

"Mind if I keep you company? I'm feeling like a ghost, wandering around this second floor."

"Hell, no. Come in. Just don't make no sudden

movements that can be seen through the open window. Here, crawl over, and you can sit up against the wall next to me."

Finally seated, she lit a cigarette. "Will this bother anything?"

"Naw," Long John answered.

"Think everything'll be okay?"

"I guess," he said. "Our luck's been holding pretty good so far. Everything's been so crazy since we came here, I don't know what's going on. I'm sort of faking it, you know? The guy who said truth is stranger than fiction really knew what he was talking about."

"Sorry you came?" Irene asked.

Long John laughed. "What *the* hell kind of a question is that? You think I like all that's happening?"

Irene didn't smile, nor did she look at Long John. "I was kind of hoping you were glad you met me."

He looked long at Irene. His voice was soft. "Sure, I'm glad I met you."

"I'm glad I met you, too," she said.

There was a moment of silence between them, then Irene laughed. "Listen to us, we sound like a couple of kids: 'I like you, do you like me?' It's all very unseemly in the North Blue Room of Eros Ranch." She couldn't hide the bitterness. "You're a john—no pun intended—and I'm what is charitably known as a hostess. What a down."

Long John didn't respond to her bitterness. "Not such a down," he said. "I've been a lot further down." He looked for words as though they were hidden under the doormat. "Maybe things ain't what they were two

nights ago. Things change people, you know? I seen it
lots. Guy gets in a war, or a bad accident, or something,
and he comes out different. Things ain't the same with
us either. Least that's how I figure it. Yeah, I really
like you."

"Whore with the heart of gold, huh?"

Another long pause. "Maybe I like you better'n you
think. Seems like you're wasting a lot of time hating
yourself. Why fight if there's no one in the ring with
you?"

"Sorry. It sounds like self-pity, doesn't it? After all,
nobody put a gun to my head and drove me here," Irene
said. "I don't hate myself. I've always been quite ade-
quate for my own purposes." Pause. "Before this. Right
now I'd like to be something different, something you
could like. Shall we fly in the face of all that's hip and
trendy? Shall we use a dumb word like *respect?* I wish I
were something you could respect. How's that for
spilling your guts?"

"Look, Renie, I ain't a guy who's good with words.
Never have been. I been kicking around the ashcans
most of my life, and if I don't say things right, you just
take it into account. Sure you were pretty when I first
saw you, and sure I wanted to make it with you. That
ain't no sin, is it? I didn't start *liking* you till after the
night in the cabin. You know what I mean?

"And who the hell am I not to respect you? I been
around. I done some pretty wild things, too. Everybody
does what they can. If you work in a—at Eros Ranch,
that's your business.

"Watching you checking in them bodies, I said to

myself, 'Man, that's one hell of a woman.' Anyhow, that's what I mean."

Irene's voice was as thin as a reed. "Thanks," she said.

Long John turned his eyes to the grass again for a minute. "Maybe I'm a little bit scared of you."

Irene's eyes opened.

"I don't figure you," Long John said. "You ain't like the rest of us. Like the big guy or me, or like Katie or Candy. You don't talk like we do. You talk more like the two docs. You sound like you might have been to college."

"I was. Class of '74. English major." Irene smiled a nice smile. "Want to know what a nice girl like me is doing in a place like this?"

"Now, look . . ."

"Sorry. I couldn't resist." She touched his arm. She laughed and sat back against the wall. "Oh God. I used to think that was a gag, but they really do say it. I came up with all kinds of answers. 'I'm doing research for a book called *Nice Girl in a Place Like This*; I'm waiting for a bus to Hollywood'; Or 'Isn't this Jackie O's party?' "

The laugh died down. She became pensive again.

"You really want to know?" she asked.

"Sure."

"No sad stories. I promise. On second thought, I don't think I'll tell you at all. Not that I'm afraid you wouldn't understand. I'm afraid *I* don't understand. It has to do with knowing how to fold a napkin and knowing which side of a calling card to bend down, the not having anyplace to practice. Does that all make sense? I don't think so. I was raised to be a perfect Victorian lady by two people who wanted me to be just like their mothers. Funny thing: I walked out of the house and found it was the twentieth century." Again the bitter laughter.

"Calling cards?" asked Long John, clearly puzzled.

"Anyway. Since Mummy and Daddy trained me to cope with a world that didn't exist, I decided to create my own world. Now I worry about birth control pills."

Long John was silent.

"You don't understand," she said.

"Maybe not. My life was never that complicated."

Almost defensively she said, "I always had the feeling Daddy betrayed me. Somehow." She dragged on her cigarette. "I went to Hollywood and found out that Hollywood doesn't exist either. I got a job as an assistant to the assistant contract writer. Daddy used to brag about his brilliant daughter. If he was so proud of me, what the hell did he ever do to help?"

"He sent you to college. That helped, didn't it?"

"Okay. I deserved that, I guess."

"I don't know," Long John said. "Maybe people who never went to college put a lot more stock in it than people that did. My old man was always on my ass to go to college on the G.I. Bill."

"How come you didn't, if it's any of my business?"

"Oh," he laughed. "Nothing serious. Ol' Big Jim and me were just too busy having fun. Next thing you know, we were over thirty."

"You love him very much, don't you?" Irene asked.

"Who him? I ain't sure I'd put it like that," Long John laughed uncomfortably at using the word *love* about another man. "But we been kicking around a long time together. He's a good ol' sonofabitch. Great guy to have around."

"You were right a while ago when you said we've all changed. You were right not understanding about my life. You're smarter than I am."

"I wouldn't say that," said Long John.

"I would. You've been in the war. You and Big Jim work on all kinds of crazy, dangerous jobs. You seem to thrive on danger. So you've learned about reality. When your life is in danger it's the only important thing. If you lose it, you lose everything. Not too many people ever learn that until it's too late. I know I've learned—finally. I'll never be the same again."

It was Irene's turn to tilt her face away. "I want you to know that when we get out of this. I'm leaving 'the business.' I'm going back to L.A. I'm not sure what I'll do. Back to writing maybe. But I won't do this anymore. And I'll *live*."

"That's good," said Long John.

"I mean it. And I want you to know it. It's important to me. Because," her voice dropped, "I want to see you again."

"I guess you will," he said. "I'd kind of like to see you again, too."

"Johnny, suppose we don't get out?" Her voice was low and soft.

"We will. I ain't dead yet, and I ain't planning to start now."

"I'm afraid we won't. I don't want my life to stop right now." She was silent for a while. "Johnny?"

"Yeah?"

"If you were to make love to me now, would it be different from the other night? I mean . . ."

"I know what you mean. Yeah. It would be different."

"Would you like to?" she asked. "I want you to. I need you. I know I'm not so pretty with the bruises and everything."

"You're pretty," he said huskily.

Long John stood up and offered her his hand. "Come on," he said. Together they went to the bed.

"Wait a minute," she added. "Lock the door."

Costaign sat alone in the bar, quietly, meditatively. He sipped a highball glass filled with brandy; he was being clubbed by it. His mind was already feeling loose as his thoughts dodged around corners and hid under the furniture.

He felt lonely now, and in the suddenly clear, unwavering reflection of the mirror, he realized the loneliness had always been there. For the first time he could pinpoint what was wrong with his life at the Sunburst. It hadn't been his practice of medicine at all. It was that everything was temporary, nothing remained in your life for more than one night. Especially, *nobody*. It was no more a real world in the hotel than it was a real world in the carnival down at Cherakowa. Perhaps he could have gotten some feeling of accomplishment from his medicine, had he been doing something with continuity. Not at the hotel.

Maybe the sheriff was like that. Maybe he survived being alone because he believed so deeply in his mission as a cop; certainly Costaign had felt that during their talk. Long John and Big Jim had each other. Even the women who had worked at Eros had each other.

Then there was Pat. She was a strange one. When she stepped out of her car yesterday, he figured her for a real pain in the ass. That had changed. She had changed. Did she, too, feel the same kind of emptiness he did?

Perhaps it was tied up with medicine—aspiring to a pinnacle that seemed so far in the distance, yet when you arrived, its familiarity and banality set you back on your ass.

"Oh, there you are. I've been looking for you," Pat said, walking to the bar. She sat on the stool next to him and touched his arm, sending a shock through him.

"You've come to the right man. And if you want to talk to me, you couldn't find a better guy." He held his breath, hoping she wouldn't remove her hand.

Pat tilted her head. "Have you been drinking?"

"No, ma'am. Present tense. *Am* drinking."

He rose and went around to the back of the bar as she followed him with her eyes. "I'm drinking cognac. Why don't you join me? It's Hennessy VSB. Very Special Brand. Or Blend. But rest assured, it's very special."

"Thank you," Pat said, strangely quiet, observing him as he placed a full glass before her.

"Don't think of it as booze," Costaign continued, "think of it as a psychological analgesic designed to relieve the effects of Armageddon. You see, my time at the Sunburst hasn't been wasted. Note the advantages of having a physician work the bar. Entertainment, relaxation, and therapy all at the same time." He shuddered as he belted back the remainder in his glass. "Having nightmares? Lost in a pit of cockroaches? Being shot at by Hell's Angels? Office hours: twenty-four hours a day."

Pat sipped her cognac. She enjoyed the caressing warmth in her stomach more than she wanted to admit. She looked at Costaign and tried to sort out the changes she saw. He was drunk, of course. Still, something had risen from inside him, something more mature. His face had become more angular, as though his teeth were clamped together, emphasizing his jaw muscles. His eyes were narrower. The skin beneath his eyes displayed tiny wrinkles she hadn't noticed before.

A strange face. On the surface it seemed to be typically American, yet beneath it, moving like undercurrents in a still pond, you could almost see the paternal line of French that had come to South and Mezo America years ago, that had intermarried with the Spaniards and the Indians. Good living had softened the face, but the hardness was only a shadow underneath.

His voice had changed. His choice of words. When she had met him, he had been a polished hotel doctor, speaking a language of bright clichés.

"I think I know what's bothering you," she said.

"Is something bothering me?"

"Yes," Pat said evenly. "Are you surprised I know?"

"I didn't think we'd agreed anything was bothering me. Up to this point, it's still your hypothesis."

Pat leaned her elbows on the bar. "Oh, yes, you just found out you weren't the big man you thought you were." She sipped again.

"Now I understand," he said. "You are a practitioner of instant psychotherapy."

"Why don't you ask me *how* I know?" she said.

Costaign's banter stopped. He leaned on the bar, his face no more than twelve inches from hers. She remained motionless.

"I'd rather find out *who* you are. If I found that out, I might be able to figure out what you are, and how you know." He leaned back against the bottle shelves. "Of course, we could always throw up our defenses again. We've been doing that. First I hated you for it. Then I found out I was as bad as you are. The defenses kept going around and around. You and I should have more in common than any two other people in this house, except for maybe Big Jim and Long John, and yet we are total strangers."

Costaign expected her to get huffy and stalk away from the bar. She didn't move.

"You're sick of being alone, aren't you?" Pat asked. "You built your own little world and you defended it against everybody. Then you found out it got pretty lonely in there."

Costaign looked amazed.

"Bright, aren't I?" she smiled ironically.

Costaign slugged from the glass. "Go on," he said, "you're doing fine." He sounded almost sober.

"You're a very attractive man. And I think you know it. I think you've had women and good times falling over you for years. I think you had a dream about being a doctor. I think you gave up that dream when you found out how being a doctor in a glamorous place like the Sunburst Hotel made you desirable. It was one big fantasy land. Then you came here and had your first brush with reality. And now you've got to rearrange all your thinking."

"Like how?"

"Oh, like finally understanding that all the people you knew before, all the glamorous people, are fun, but that there is no substance to them. When push came to shove, and your life was in danger, you found strength with a lot of people you didn't even think you'd like. They made you not only compare your friends to them, they made you compare yourself to them."

"Wow," said Costaign, shaking his head in disbelief. "You, too?"

"Oh, no. The exact opposite. I was never good-looking."

"You? Not good-looking? I think . . ." he interrupted.

"Maybe I don't stop clocks today the way I did when I was a teenager. I might have grown up to my face a little. I can assure you that when I was in school I was besieged neither by men nor good times. From there on the story becomes familiar. I began to hate all my girl friends because they could easily get the men I used to ream about. Then I began that great old self-delusion hat my life was more important than to be wasted on oth boys and foolishness. So I was to save the world vith my knowledge of medicine. As time went by, I egan to hate everybody. In fact, I felt infinitely uperior to everybody.

"This place, last night, this morning, taught me differently. I don't hate anybody. And I certainly am ot superior to anybody. I guess I learned that nobody an be alone and survive. If it hadn't been for the gang f us, not one of us would be alive today. End of story."

Costaign reached out and touched her hand. Again he didn't move.

"I've had a marvelous thought about all this," she continued. "You and I must be hardcore cases. Don't ou know what everybody else in this house has had hat we've never had? Enemies. We never before had a ife and death situation with an enemy. Oh, there's the OR. We try to fight death in there. But we've got it sanitized. We're scientific about it. When it wins, it takes somebody else's life, not ours.

"Only you and I, Bob, have never faced an enemy. When we did it turned out to be the oldest enemy mankind has, except death. Cockroaches. Did you know that? Did you know there are two thousand two hundred and fifty separate species? Did you know they've been around two hundred and fifty thousand years? They've been the enemy since we all lived in caves. They're the only enemy we've never beaten."

Bob's mouth stretched into a smile. He stared at Pat and saw a beautiful woman.

Silent, apparently emptied by her monologue, Pa
tried to read his face.

"Look at us," he said firmly. "What a couple o
winners we are!"

Pat's eyes continued to tap his face like a blind man'
fingers. Uncomprehending.

"Don't you see? You and me," he continued, "with
our gorgeous scientific minds. Here we are poking
around deep inside ourselves. We trust each other
enough to show more intimate things to each other
than we've ever shown anybody else." His voice was
low and gentle.

Suddenly, he looked away and snorted. "Did you
hear what you just said about the species of roaches
and how many years they've been around? Good God
For just one incredible minute there, it all made sense
to me!"

Bob almost doubled over with laughter. There was a
shade of hysteria about it as he slapped his hand
against his thigh, taking two steps away. "But cockroaches!"

He turned back to Pat. She saw the joke. Her face
beamed. Her fingers lightly touched her lips as she
giggled like a little girl who'd just heard a naughty
story.

It was a moment of giddy helplessness. As the laughter slowly faded, their eyes remained together. They
knew they had stepped on new ground—neither had
ever experienced before. The laughs faded away, but
each knew that somehow there was a further step to

ke. The joy of their faces became tinged with uncertainty.

Pat and Bob moved toward each other, but their feet seemed not to carry them. Pat wondered what she should do, but she didn't have time to really think about it before they were in each other's arms.

The kiss was so desperate it hurt. Free at last of their awkwardness, their hands searched, their bodies rubbed. Gentle, soothing. No technique, no style—just opposite ends of a magnetic spectrum coming together for the first time unrestrained.

After a minute, Bob and Pat were both panting like teenagers. Passion like this was still too new to be recognized, so they didn't speak. They simply looked at each other in disbelief . . . and compassion. Bob's gaze then drifted up toward the ceiling to the second floor, where the bedrooms were. Pat followed it, lowered her eyes and nodded.

His hand searched till it found hers. He slowly brought it to his mouth and kissed it.

"Pat, I . . ."

"Sshhh, I know how you . . ." she began, but Bob's mouth was already covering hers.

It was a couple of seconds before either realized what was happening. At first, joints creaked, then wood screamed against wood. Plaster walls and ceilings split with fork-lightning fissures. Windowpanes buckled, then shattered. The whole house pitched as though it were being worried between the jaws of a giant dog. In

one cataclysmic moment, the house roared and settled
to one side, the garage side. The floor heaved, tossing
tables and chairs, rolling furniture, and bringing two
nineteenth-century chandeliers booming to the floor

CHAPTER
FOURTEEN

Costaign and Pat dragged themselves up from the floor where they had been hurled. The room was clouded with dust as they blindly picked their way through the jumble of furniture that pressed against the bar, obeying the law of gravity on the tilting floor. They coughed and tried to shield their eyes. Finally, they staggered out to the parlor.

There, too, it was dark. The air was thick with the smell of dry plaster, dust as thick as an Okie's nightmare. They could see a partial outline of the sheriff against a front window.

"Anybody hurt!" he was shouting. "Sing out! Anybody hurt?"

Costaign and Pat answered first. Then Big Jim and Katie, working their way from the storeroom at the back, under the stairs. Long John and Irene called from the second floor.

"That's everybody," the sheriff said. "Good thing we were all on this side of the house when she went."

The dust, boiling out through the shattered windows and doors, quickly emptied out of the room.

"Looks like we were right, Doc," Big Jim said to Pat. "We ain't got eight hours."

"We gotta get out of this place right now," said the sheriff. "Thank God the right side of the building is still in shape."

Long John and Irene stumbled down from the second floor. "What the hell happened?" asked Long John.

"The roaches," Big Jim answered. "Man, I knew they were undermining the house, but I didn't know it was this bad. The whole goddam foundation on the garage side just gave."

"How can that be?" Katie was stunned. "Roaches don't do things like that. I mean, I thought it was termites."

"These aren't the same kind of roaches you get in your apartment," Pat said. "These are the big outdoor kind. They didn't actually eat at the house, they were breeding underground and simply loosened all the dirt out from under the foundation."

"Well, we ain't got too much time to sit around," said the sheriff. "We gotta get moving right now. Couple more minutes and the whole place will be down around our ears. We got to make our move."

"At the rate they're breeding, they may not wait until dark to come up for food," Pat added.

A sense of urgency sprang up among them.

"So what do we do?" Big Jim asked. "Same plan? Go out to the hill coming down from the mountain? Try to find the old water cut?"

"I don't see nothing else," said the sheriff.

"Me, neither. We sure as hell can't get past that Caddy. How do we handle the guy who's guarding the water cut?"

Pat jumped in. "We have to get out as soon as we can. And I think we have to take whatever chances we need." Everyone in the room, white-faced from the settling dust, looked at her. "We have a bigger problem on our hands than just saving our own lives. Somebody has to get out. It's these roaches. Someone has to get in touch with the health department so we can start extermination as soon as possible. The roaches are breeding at a tremendous rate. There must be trillions of them already. Try to imagine if they spread out over the state. Suppose they were to attack a town the way they attacked us last night.

"At least now they're all in one place. If we're ever going to get them, we have to get them here. If we don't, it could be the beginning of a new plague."

Costaign shuddered to think of the possibilities.

"I guess that settles it," said Big Jim. "You're right, Doc, they might come up here looking for food long before sunset."

Banzo was alone behind the convertible. He gripped

his rifle even tighter as he scrutinized the hacienda. He was feeling alone. He had just begun to ease out of another of his wrenching headaches. In the silence since the hot-blooded action had died down, a few facts were taking shape. Carmine and Ritter were dead. Even if they got the sheriff, they'd already paid two for one.

Boris had split. Patton should be holding down behind the wood building near where the house had collapsed. Bird on the other side. Cutter had been kind of funny. He had looked at Banzo a few minutes ago, had said something about going to the bathroom, and had disappeared into the trees. He hadn't returned. Banzo wondered if he had split, the way Boris had. It looked like there were only three of them left.

He studied the crazy angle of the hacienda. Man, that was nuts, a house falling like that. What made it fall? Obviously nobody'd been hurt. He had waited to hear screams. There had been some surprised shouting, but no screams.

Banzo didn't know what to do. He knew he couldn't wait around forever. The threat of the roaches now seemed directed at all of them. What about Carmine? Maybe he had taken off, too. Everything was foggy. For all he knew, it could be just him and Bird.

He knew one thing: The sheriff was still there, and he was going to get him. The fiery anger in his gut had turned to an obsession. Banzo suddenly saw the gully as a great arena. Either he or the sheriff was going to die here. It didn't matter what anybody else did.

"Hey, Sheriff!" Banzo called. "When you coming out?

ou ain't gonna hide forever! Come on out and get it
ver!"

A tiny smile played the sheriff's lips. What the
ikers had originally intended as psychological pressure
n the people in the house was now beginning to work
n reverse. Whitney could detect the heavy edginess in
he biker's voice. He knew he was winning the standoff.

Since Pat had voiced her concern about the roaches,
he group was packing up. There was no panic among
hem, only the feeling that circumstances were now
orcing them to move faster than they anticipated.
Shit, the sheriff thought. Those roaches. This house.
He was convinced that if only they had enough time,
hey could resolve the duel with the bikers and *walk*
ut of there.

Only the sheriff and Costaign remained at the door.
The women had gone in search of stronger clothes,
perhaps jeans that might be laying around. All were so
scratched up already, they wanted to avoid what the
brush country would do to their bodies if they fled. Big
Jim and Long John had gone to search out the weapons
Irene was convinced they wouldn't find.

The sheriff's face was fixed as he kept his vigil.

"Are we going to make it?" the doctor asked, trying
to keep fear out of his voice.

"Our luck keeps holding out and we will. Pity this
house won't hold up for a while."

"It won't be easy though?" Costaign insisted.

"Nothing's easy, Doc. This Banzo didn't turn out to
be as smart as I give him credit for; but he's tough."

"You've got a strange expression on your face, Sheriff. You look for all the world like a fellow who doesn't care whether he gets out of here."

Whitney turned his eyes to Costaign for the briefest moment, then returned them to his vigil.

"What have I got to be so happy about? Except being alive. If I get out with my skin, I'm lucky. You know what the whole story is and you know what's going to happen to me when I get out."

Costaign nodded.

"I'm going to have to give a lot of answers to a lot of people. You know what all this is going to sound like in the newspapers and on TV, don't you? You know what an investigating committee is going to do with me?" Whitney finished.

Costaign was silent. He knew the sheriff was right. As with everything else since he arrived at Eros, Costaign's feelings about the sheriff had changed. He knew a situation that may have started out innocently enough had gotten out of the sheriff's control.

"You know, Sheriff, you didn't have to come back to this gulley and get yourself mixed up with those bikers. You did that for us. To make sure we were all right."

The sheriff's eyes showed gratitude. "If it hadn't been for me, you wouldn't have been here in the first place," Whitney said.

"I think you've got six friends here," Costaign offered.

Their conversation was snapped off. A sudden, high-pitched scream rolled across the lawn. It seemed to ome from the right. Keeping down, and keeping the amb between himself and Banzo, the sheriff flung the oor open.

"What's that?" a voice called from upstairs.

The scream reverberated again and again around he gulley wall.

"Jesus, look!" gasped the sheriff.

Costaign saw the hill over which they intended to scape shiver for a moment, then with a sigh, collapse. rom the base to a hundred yards up, a boiling cloud of ust rose as a sizable avalanche crumbled down to fill he vacuum created by the caved-in earth. Tons of dirt kidded down. A cloud of dust rolled across the lawn. Vith the avalanche, mixed in with the dirt, were undreds of thousands of cockroaches. Clawing and umbling, rolling, skittering, and squidging!

The rest of the group ran into the parlor to join Costaign and Whitney. They took positions behind the hattered windows as the tableau of hell continued utside. Suddenly, a figure emerged into view: It was he biker who had been guarding the water cut. He was maddened animal, running, screaming hysterically vhile his hands flailed at his body.

"Take cover! Bird, for Christ's sake!" Banzo screamed.

The young biker heard nothing. He had been churned under the earth. He had seen blackness in broad day-ight. He had been swallowed by the blackness, then egurgitated. Fiends swarmed and clawed him. He ould experience no greater terror.

"Halt! This is the police!" Whitney shouted the bligatory warning.

The young man continued to run, throwing his head from side to side, bellowing. A burst of gunfire from Banzo's M-16 thwitted harmlessly into the doorjamb.

"Fuck, Sheriff!" Banzo shrieked. "Don't you see . . ."

The sheriff squeezed off one round. The young man was smashed sideways and flung to the ground. The dust rolled over him like a tide.

"You no good sonofabitch!" Banzo screamed.

The sheriff was rigidly alert, facing Banzo.

"Come on. One more time, sonny boy. Blow your cool," the sheriff whispered aloud.

Another burst of automatic fire sent splinters flying around the door.

"No you don't, you bastard!" Banzo's voice called out. "You ain't suckering me!"

The sheriff relaxed. It was a cruelty to gun down the unarmed biker madly fleeing the roaches and the disappearing earth. But the sheriff used the tactic to lure Banzo from behind the convertible so he could get a clear shot at him. It didn't work.

A week ago, the group in the room would have been horrified. Today, they had lived too long on the fine line of extinction to be greatly shocked.

"That's the break we been waiting for. The north side's clear now," said Long John. "Let's get the hell out of here!"

CHAPTER
FIFTEEN

"You guys get going. I'll hold Banzo off till you're clear," the sheriff said.

"How will you get out?" Pat asked.

"Don't worry. You just take off. You worry about finding a path around them roaches."

"Hey, lookee lookee," said Big Jim, grinning. He jiggled a brown paper bag. Turning the bag upside down, five dynamite sticks slipped into his other hand. "Maybe we'll have something to cover you with."

"Christ! Where'd you find those?" the sheriff asked.

"In the maintenance shop out back. Here," said Big Jim, "you take a couple of these." He dropped two sticks into the sheriff's lap. "We'll split. Soon's we're out, you toss one of these things in pretty boy's face,

then come running. One of us'll be covering you from
the corner of the house. Okay?"

"You got it," said Whitney.

"In case we're on the move when you get there," said
Long John, "we'll be going straight up the hill till we
get clear of where the roaches are, then cut over to the
spillway. There's a macadam path that runs from the
house to the hillside. You just follow the path and go
right up the hill."

"Gotcha," said Whitney.

The group, in this instant of liberation, although
their souls were leaping like puppy dogs, suddenly fell
silent. As though they couldn't believe the moment had
really come. Grins were frozen on their lips. They
looked at each other as though waiting for someone to
renounce this final, great act.

"For Christ's sake, go!" the sheriff said.

"See you in the woods, Sheriff," said Costaign.

They clattered off, leaving the sheriff at his post.

The afternoon sun baked the earth. The stinging
smell that filled the air was not only desert dryness,
but the heavy redolence of new-churned soil.

The side door of the house was a great wood portal
fashioned in the old Mexican style. Bordered with blue
and white tile, it stood at the end of a heavy-beamed
hallway.

The door was flung open. Pat, Costaign, Big Jim, and
Katie were crouched outside behind a low wall of hedge
that followed the path from the door to the hillside,
where both the hedge and the path joined a broad walk

that curved around to the front of the house. Long John and Irene stood just inside the door, out of sight of the others.

He pressed her tightly against the wall and kissed her. It was a quick, unexpected move. She struggled for a minute, then gave in.

"Johnny, please. We have to . . ."

"You know what?" he smiled. "I really like skinny broads."

Irene grinned. "Come on, let's go," she said. "Plenty of time for that later."

As she spoke, the air split with the deep-throated roar of a dynamite explosion. It bounced off the walls of the gulley and rolled back. It sent shock waves through the ground.

"That's it!" Big Jim called, and the four outside were on their feet.

Irene and Long John swung out through the door. Without warning, they were in the center of a shower of crashing wood and stone. Irene's scream was lost in the rumble as the side of the house crashed down on them!

The other four stopped about a third of the way down the path.

"Oh, no," moaned Katie, seeing the side of the house split clear up to the roof.

They raced back, digging frantically in the debris, ignoring the blinding dust.

"Here," Costaign called, at last. "Over here."

Big Jim was like a mechanical device, an insane engine. He grunted as his massive bulk rolled and pitched the chunks of adobe that covered his friend. Costaign worked next to him. The bodies were finally uncovered.

"Wait a minute, Big Jim," Costaign gasped from the exertion, "let me have a look at them."

The big man stood back. His fists clenched. His face twisted.

With Irene, it had been simple. A huge beam, possibly the support for the door, had struck her head full force. She had died instantly. The beam had then, under the pressure of other debris, rolled down her chest, pulverizing her rib cage. Her face, under its coating of dust, looked like a Kabuki death mask.

"John's alive," Costaign said. Big Jim swiftly bent over the prostrate body. Alive, yes. That's the most that could be said. His breath was as tattered as an old sail. With each exhalation, a spurt of blood bubbled from his mouth. The same beam that had crushed Irene lay immobile across his belly.

"Oh Jesus, oh Jesus," It was a chant of animal agony torn out from Jim's throat. He saw the weight on his friend, the pile of stone, and he knew. He gently dusted the whiteness from Long John's face; his own face, he blotted with the back of the other hand.

"He's alive," Big Jim said.

"His lungs," Costaign said, "are . . ."

"Fuck that! He's alive." Even as Big Jim said the words, the ineluctable process began under his hand. The skin of his friend began to wax over; beneath the fingernails, the pale oilyness of death.

"He's gone, Big Jim," said Costaign, louder than he

ight have, but he had to keep his voice from cracking.

Big Jim knew. He had seen the process before.

"Hey, long fellow. Hey, listen to me. Can you hear
e?" Big Jim said.

And for the first time, Long John did not answer.

Big Jim began tearing wildly at the debris that cov-
red his friend. Costaign gripped his shoulder and
eld.

"Goddamit! Don't just stand there! You're a doctor.
)o something. That's Long John lying there!"

The persistence of Costaign's grip seemed to slowly
vaken Big Jim. He stopped heaving slowly, like a
vound-down clock. Slowly, he straightened up, but his
yes never left his friend's face. It was filmed over. The
ips had withdrawn from the teeth. Big Jim gave up.

Side by side, Long John and Irene lay dead in the
errible dust.

Big Jim stood quietly. There were no tears in his
eyes. The earth did not stop in its orbit. The sun did not
;o out, nor did the stars plunge. Everything was
exactly the same—except a tall, skinny guy from San
Francisco named Long John Markley was dead.

A burst of gunfire sputtered around the other side of
he house.

His hand still on Big Jim's shoulder, Costaign
whispered, "We have to go."

"You go. I'm staying here," said Big Jim, his voice
expressionless.

"You can't . . ." Costaign began.

"Bet your ass I can. I'm not leaving him for no
fucking cockroaches."

Katie, her face shifting expressions, stepped up to the other side of Big Jim and took his hand.

"I know," she said.

Big Jim just turned his head to her.

"I'll stay with you. Irene was my friend. I had no idea we weren't going to get out of this," she said.

"You can't stay, kid. I'll take care of this myself."

Katie could no longer speak. She shook her head.

"Don't be a jerk," Big Jim growled.

The woman clung to his arm and continued shaking her head.

Standing in back of him, Pat spoke. "She's right, Big Jim, either we all go, or none of us do."

Another exchange of gunfire rattled from the front of the house and reignited the feeling of urgency in them. Big Jim seemed to come back to himself. The blankness left his face; his features returned to their normal set. His attention swept in one elliptical arc from the fire fight between Banzo and Whitney to Katie to Costaign and Pat to the bodies of Long John and Irene.

He nodded to Katie. He looked one final time at Long John. "So long, chief," he said, making a sound that only a wounded cat could make. He turned to the others. "Let's go."

With Big Jim leading the way, the four took off for the hillside.

A hundred and fifty yards up, thirty yards over, they found the water cut. It was ugly and overgrown: a trench ten feet wide, three or four feet deep. The mountain country of Nevada is riven with such fissures,

hough the stranger's eye barely discerns them. His
ttention is directed to them only by periodic signs:
Vatch for Flash Floods.

Big Jim stood in the center of the trench, looking
pward toward the lake.

"This is it," he said to his companions.

Banzo knew, at last, that he was alone. He kept the
tock of the M-16 pressed into the hollow of his
houlder. He narrowed all his concentration into the
ingle task of his duel with the sheriff. Although he
ook comfort from the weight of the ammunition
emaining in his pockets, and he kept the selector
witch on *full automatic*, he no longer intended to
pray his fire as he had. He, like the sheriff, would pick
is targets.

The sheriff's cover fire hadn't fooled him. He knew
hey were up to something in there. He guessed the
ther people in the house were on the move. Let 'em go.
Ie wasn't after them. But where would they go? The
orth hill. Where else? Any other move and he would
ave spotted them.

He felt his headache starting again. The pains began
t his eyes and shot around his temples. This one was
;oing to be a bitch. Goddamit. It had to come now when
ne needed all his wits about him. The sheriff and he
vere dealing out the last hand. He was afraid he would
nake the fatal slip. The fact is, Banzo had already
nade the fatal slip: He had not paid attention to the
nature of the arena in which he fought. His concentra-
:ion had been too great.

He did not consider why the house might have crum bled, nor did he seem aware of the humming lif beneath him, the ground that shifted, the gulley wall that were gradually sinking into darkness.

"Hey, Sheriff!" he called. "It's you and me now. M people are all gone. Your people are gone, too. Now I'r gonna get you. I'll do it any way you want. Just yo and me. What do you say?"

An object, looking like an overgrown firecracke lobbed out the door, flipping end over end. Banz ducked his head. The earth trembled beneath him. I front of him, a geyser lifted into the air. When i settled, Banzo called again. "Fuck you, chicken shit That dynamite ain't gonna save you. Time to chang tactics, right? If I can't get you, I get them people o yours!"

Banzo spun away from his position behind the con vertible and raced in a low crouch, back to the trees

"Did you hear him?" Katie said. "He's coming afte us!"

Big Jim, who stood next to her against the rise of the gulley, answered only, "Yeah," but his eyes moved up and down the water cut. He held tight to the paper bag which contained his share of the dynamite sticks. Pat began to tremble. Out in the open, away from the house, she felt naked and vulnerable.

Costaign understood. Holding her hand, he could feel her shudder. It was also the knowledge that the sheriff no longer stood between them and the biker. Whatever they did, they'd have to do on their own. Thinking of this, and of Irene's and Long John's death, the feeling of liberation they had experienced a little while ago turned to ashes.

"Maybe we'd better get started and let Whitney catch up with us," Costaign said.

"Can't," said Big Jim. "Somebody's got to guide him in. He don't know where the split in the ground is, and he don't know where the roaches are. You go. You take the girls. I got to wait."

"We can't leave you," Pat said.

"I'm not going without you," said Katie.

"Hang in then. Find some cover in case that biker maniac starts shooting. Keep your eye out for the sheriff."

From their position, the trees were too thick to allow them a view of the lawn.

"I sure hope he hurries," said Katie.

Anton Whitney knew Banzo would make his move then. After his threat, he heard Banzo scoot away from the car. He chanced leaning out the door to get a better look, holding his weapon in firing position.

The sheriff tried to imagine which way the biker would go to reach the area where his friends were making their escape. Simple, he thought: through the trees to the cabins, from the cabins through the little cluster of mobile homes, then along the base of the forward cliff to the water cut. Banzo would have cover clear up to the north slope. Even there the sheriff wouldn't be able to get at him because the avalanche and roaches were between here and there. It seemed to him he had no choice but to join his friends on the slope.

The sheriff had used his ammunition sparingly, so there was no concern on that score. As long as it had been a duel between the sheriff and Banzo his marksmanship and hitting power had equalized Banzo's automatic weapons. Those advantages were now gone.

Almost immediately, Whitney's theory was confirmed, as he saw a dark figure dart from the edge of the grove into the area of the mobile homes.

For the first time all day, Whitney was free to leave his post at the door. He clumped through the debris of the parlor, on his way to the north door. He worked his way into the bar, where the floor was as uneven as the surface of the ocean. From the bar, he ducked into the hallway leading to the door. Both sides of the hall were lined with rooms in which the ghosts from the graveyard bar had acted out their fantasies of love or sex. They contrasted like double exposures against the reality of tattered curtains and besotted beds, lace garments which lay as empty as the discarded husks of the roaches.

The end of the world, he thought, will be something like this.

Whitney pulled up short as he approached the collapsed doorway.

"Oh, no," he agonized, discovering Irene's and Long John's lifeless bodies. Covered with dust, they might have been ghosts from the bar.

He ran the length of the path, hitting the woods at

full tilt. He struggled up the hill. He wondered how far he'd have to climb before he was above the line of roaches. A few minutes later, puffing, his face flushed from the exertion, he took a chance and cut over.

He froze when he heard his name called, until he realized it was not the voice of Banzo.

"It's me, Sheriff, Dr. Costaign."

With gratitude, a few minutes later, he piled into the water cut with his friends. There were smiles all around. But not for long.

A spray of automatic fire hissed through the trees.

"You people better get going, he's after you," the sheriff said.

"Yeah, we know. We heard him. Good thing you got here first with that cannon," said Big Jim. "Now we can get out. Doc, you take the chicks and start up the spillway. We'll fall back after you. All we have to do is let that sonofabitch know we're here. That'll slow him up, and we'll all meet at the top."

"But . . ." Kate began.

"Go, babe," Big Jim said. "No bullshit this time. The sheriff and me'll take care of this guy. He's alone now, and we're armed. We'll be right up after you. Now, go, will you, and quit wasting time."

Costaign began collecting the women with a deep feeling of satisfaction. For the first time since he had come to this satanic gulley, he realized he was not moving out of fear. He had made the same inner adjustments that Long John and Big Jim and Whitney had made. He felt he could now trust his own courage.

"Big Jim is right," he said. He looked to Pat. She smiled and seemed to understand. "We'll just give that psychotic more targets if we hang around."

"That's right, Doc," the sheriff said.

Costaign and the three women began the long trek up the water cut. Katie looked back at Big Jim. "See you later?" she asked.

"Later," said Big Jim with a smile.

"Sonofabitch!"

Banzo had been forced to take the long way around, and he knew that had given the sheriff time enough to join the others. Sonofabitch.

Where is that dude? If he's dug in, he can pick me off like a frigging fly. Easy. Take it easy. Move slowly now. Banzo remembered the sheriff's accuracy with the Magnum. He found himself choking on his fear. At any instant, he expected a bullet to crash through his chest.

He figured the others would probably take off up the mountain. The sheriff would hang behind, setting an ambush. But where would he hide? He had these woods. If Banzo did not move fast enough, if he were *too* cautious, he would lose them all. If the sheriff had time to get in touch with his deputies, everything would be gonzo for him.

He decided to duck from tree to tree, on the run, rather than creep along the ground.

Big Jim, looking over one side of the trench, waved at the sheriff, who was looking out from the other side. With his hand he indicated, "Come here."

"There he is," Big Jim whispered. "See him? Down by that outcropping. He just ducked in from the trees behind it."

The sheriff flopped next to Big Jim and pointed his pistol. Big Jim touched his arm.

Hefting one of the dynamite sticks, he said, "Give me a match, and I'll slow him up."

Whitney was sure Big Jim's powerful arm could make the distance. Big Jim touched the fuse to Whitney's proffered Zippo and lobbed it high through the trees. Both men sprawled on their faces. The red missile floated end over end, cracked into a branch, and dropped, slightly this side of the rock outcropping. Before it hit the ground it ripped the air with an orange fist, sending wood splinters whizzing like shrapnel in all directions.

"Let's go!" said Big Jim, when the last tremble of the explosion had died away.

Banzo was slammed—first by the shock of the explosion, then by the jolting force of his headache. For one moment, the pain pierced his skull like a nail. He slapped up both hands and opened his mouth in a soundless scream. A few minutes later the headache ebbed away. His hands slowly dropped to their normal position. They felt at home caressing the M-16.

He heard footsteps scrabbling away, but the rocks and scrub were a perfect screen in front of him. He tried to make up with his hearing what he lacked in vision, but the sound of the footsteps was being swallowed up.

Banzo worked his way around the rocks until he broke clear near the water cut. He felt a moment of giddy fear realizing that he was alone. A compulsion, a force with knife edges within him drove him on, even though he knew he was outnumbered. He trotted along the unvegetated rim of the gulley, heading upward

He heard the footsteps again. He squiggled into the brush, trying to maintain a sense of direction, keeping the sounds directly in front of him. It might be easier than he imagined. As he figured, the footsteps, too, were following the gulley.

His headache suddenly started again. Goddam it Not now. They were bastards, those headaches. They seemed never to go away. He had had them ever since . . . ever since . . . Christ, he couldn't remember. Whatever it was, it had been inside him a long time.

Without warning, a couple of rocks skittered down the gulley. Banzo swung the rifle in their direction, at the same time leaping toward the edge. He almost jumped into the gulley, then stopped himself. A twisting smile worked itself across his face.

Trying to sucker me, huh? Trying to make me think you're zeroed in, and that I'd better jump into that ditch for cover? Screw you. That ain't cover. That's a bowling alley. I get down into that thing and you can roll anything down on top of me. Can't miss.

Banzo, crouched and wary, continued along the rim. His arms worked in front of him, slashing away branches and twigs. Careful, he thought. That sheriff's a tricky mother, and this is the showdown. How about that for cowboy jive? His legs continued working like machines. Sweat trickled burningly into his eyes.

In one spot the course of the water cut moved into a wide arc. As he reached one tip of the arc, he caught a glimpse of them. No. Not them. Him! The sheriff. Suddenly, for the first time in his life, Banzo's mind made a clear, incisive cut into his innards, and he knew. The phantom. The figure that never came into focus. The figure that had for so many years lurked on the periphery of his brain. The figure that had driven him and driven him. The suggestion of authority, the hint of uniform. There it was before him right this moment in the flesh! The sheriff. Him and a thousand like him. The pursuers. The pushers. The oppressors. In one cataclysmic moment of comprehension he knew why he didn't run when the others had either been killed or had deserted him. Banzo now had his phantom in the open. On the run. And he had to kill it at all costs.

"Don't run, mother!" he shouted. "I gotcha, man, I gotcha!"

He clamped the M-16 against his side and sent a swarm of angry, buzzing bullets in the sheriff's direction.

Banzo's slugs kicked up thutting little geysers just a few yards away from Whitney and Big Jim. Both men dived for cover along the sides of the bend.

"Goddam," the sheriff puffed, "that sonofabitch is up to us already."

Big Jim hefted another stick of dynamite. The sheriff swung out his Magnum.

Another burst chewed up the ground. Closer this

time. They heard incoherent shouting from the biker
A second later they heard the sound of movement
Assuming Banzo had slid into the gulley, Whitney
fired a single shot in the direction of the noise. Big Jim
waiting another second, lit and lobbed the dynamite
stick.

Banzo's face was a mad laughing-mask as the dyna
mite flashed like a storm in the gulley below him
raining down dirt and pebbles. As the last quiver o
reverberating air rolled off into the surrounding hills
Banzo started to laugh; it was a maniac's laugh. I
stalked the mountain. Like an apparition it seemed to
come from no particular place, yet every place at once
"Up yours, Sheriff," Banzo shrieked. "You ain't getting me. I'm on your program!"

Pat squealed as she lost her balance and skidded
backward on her belly for a few feet. She spun over
trying to regain herself, and smacked into a large rock.
"Oh God, I've hurt my ankle," she said between
clenched teeth. "Oooh, it hurts. Damn."
One look and Costaign knew it was more than a
sprain. Already the ankle was as big as a baseball. The
skin, the color of rainbow bronze, was taut and shiny.
"We'll give you a hand with that," Costaign offered.
"We can take care of it later."
Costaign tore a couple of strips from the robe he was
wearing and bound Pat's ankle. She, too, knew it was
worse than a sprain.

"Katie, give me a hand here, will you," he asked. The two then helped Pat to her feet. "We've got to keep moving. I know it hurts. Can you do it?"

Pat nodded, and they started to move upward again. Each time her injured foot made contact with the ground, Pat's face twisted in agony.

"We'll make it, honey," Katie said. "We can't be too far from the top, can we?"

A popping of gunfire caused each of them to turn around. The air then thumped with another explosion. Their innards chilled as they heard the maniacal laughter. It seemed to increase the nightmare quality of their situation.

"Oh, c'mon, let's keep moving," Katie pleaded.

Banzo heard the sheriff pulling out again. Run, mother, he thought through his grin. As he took his first step to continue his pursuit, he was again flushed with the fear of his aloneness. How would he know if the sheriff set up an ambush? He was smart enough for that. Be careful. Be careful.

But it was hard for him to think clearly. The headache was turning into a crown of thorns. Before him, behind him, to the left, and right, the world seemed filled with pain. His laugh had been a scream, a sheer physical response to unbearable agony. He wondered how long before he did scream. He wasn't quitting now, ambush or no ambush. He moved more cautiously, deeper in his crouch, his finger tensed on the trigger.

The pain began to affect his vision. The wildness

around him became unnaturally black. Colors shifte
from black to red to gold in a single rotating band
Rocks became gaping skulls.

He cursed and prayed simultaneously in his growing
helplessness. Then he saw them again. He fired from
the hip.

"I'm hit," Whitney hissed. "Sonofabitch." One leg
suddenly sprouted a red rose of blood. He slumped.

"He's on top of us again. Here, gimme that cannon,
said Big Jim, clipping his words.

He held the weapon out in front of him with both
hands, police fashion. He could see nothing. The
shadows of afternoon were becoming the shadows of
night. He fired one round, just to keep Banzo cautious

"Hey, Doc!" Big Jim called. "Come back. The sheriff's
hit." His voice rolled up the mountain.

The maniacal laugh roared again. The sheriff bent
over, clutching the leg. Big Jim was still as a leopard
Then he saw the figure move.

A feral creature, it slithered along the rim of the
gulley. For one timeless second, it stood out clearly
black against the lightness of the sky.

Boom!

To Big Jim's vision, the creature simply vanished in
the smoke.

"Get him?" Whitney hissed, still clutching his wound.

"Can't tell. But I don't see how I could have missed."

They listened. They heard only silence.

A crab had entered Banzo's belly. It clawed and tore

him. There was now only slimy blood where his buckle should have been.

There was no expression of agony on Banzo's face, only an incongruous look of relief as the gore poured from his body. He had seen death, and he knew he was dying. He even felt the numbness in his limbs starting. One of us, he thought grimly. It didn't matter which—either him or the sheriff—it didn't matter which died, but one of them had to. It was not exactly true that Banzo wanted to die; he just wanted to be free of the poisons inside him and outside.

He rolled over on his belly, then pushed himself up on his elbows. The wound in his belly added a weight to his back. He struggled to his hands and knees, one hand still clenched firmly around the rifle. I'm a tough mama, all right, he spat. That dude's using a Magnum.

"Yeah, I'm dying. But not without you, fuzz. Payback is a motherfucker," he said aloud.

He toddled to the edge of the water cut, slowly, painfully, then he let himself slide into it. They wouldn't be looking for him there. I get one more shot, he thought, and this time you're wasted.

Again he crawled. When he reached a bend, he peered around and saw them. One was hit. The other was bending over him. The clowns. They weren't even looking. They thought they had blown him away. No way he could miss now. One shot, that's all. One burst. The weakness of death was on him.

He sighted at Big Jim's broad back.

Only the rifle and the hands that held it were visible

to Costaign, who came out in that exact instant on the rim of the bend. Before he could think, his body acted for him. He hurled himself through the air like a football tackler. He missed Banzo. But he crashed into the side of the gulley next to him, scattering dirt on the rifle and its bearer. It was enough. Banzo was flung sideways. Costaign, in a flash, sprang onto Banzo.

Big Jim and the sheriff looked up, stunned.

Costaign was on top of Banzo, flailing wildly with his fists, awkwardly pounding. Big Jim leaped to help. He tore Costaign away in an instant of comprehension. Costaign was so wild with fear, he had not noticed that the body beneath him was still. At last Costaign stood away panting.

"He's dead, Doc. For Christ's sake look at him."

"Dead, finally, you mean," said the sheriff.

"Yeah," Big Jim agreed. "I guess there was enough life in him to squeeze that trigger." Big Jim looked at Costaign who was regaining his breath. "You did good, Doc. Now see what you can do about the sheriff, will you? He's hit in the leg."

CHAPTER
SIXTEEN

ostaign and Big Jim slumped onto the ground ext to the sheriff, ostensibly to look at his wound, reality out of sheer relief. Banzo was dead. The biker ng had been either killed or run off. They were clear f the Eros Ranch compound. For the first time in fortyght hours, they were safe.

Costaign tore at the sheriff's pants leg. With eyes nd gentle fingers, he examined the wound.

"Good thing you're a big guy. The bullet doesn't seem o have hit the bone. How does it feel?"

"Like I spilled hot coffee all over myself."

"Think you can walk if we give you a hand?" said the loctor.

"Bet your ass I can. I'd run if I had enough people hasing me."

"Good man," said Costaign. "We'd better get up wit
the women as soon as we can. Pat has hurt her ankl
I'm afraid it's broken."

"Looks like ain't none of us coming out of this clean
said Big Jim.

Costaign and Big Jim helped Whitney to his fee
They opted to stay in the water cut on the way up. :
was a little rougher, but it gave greater suppor
underfoot, with its rocks and irregular ground.

Costaign remembered the moment when he ha
stood on the ridge overlooking the Eros compounc
When was it? Yesterday? *Only yesterday?* He remem
bered the full view of Eros sitting like a little toy towr
The entire gulley looking like a hole in the ground. H
wondered what they, the survivors, must look lik
crawling out of a pit.

The deepening darkness set off an alarm in then
that made them hurry. Would they ever be able t
stand the onset of night again?

They continued to climb upward, even symbolicall\
a physical indication their travail was over. From th
gathering dusk of earth they moved only in the directior
of the still-brilliant sky. Soon, perhaps, there would be
thoughts and evaluations; for the moment, only the
irresistible pull of freedom, at the top of the mountain

They rounded a turn and saw the women, whose
faces lit up like a brightening sun. They called, they
waved. The men, puffing, answered.

"It's over!" Costaign croaked. "Banzo's dead!"

The sheriff and Big Jim smiled to each other through
their sweat.

Their smiles froze as a sound reached their ears. It started as a rumble, almost a cat's purr, deep in the earth. The three men stopped, turned in the direction of the ranch, and lifted their heads as though testing the wind. The rumble seemed to move beneath their feet. It might have been a bowling ball lumbering slowly along a subterranean alley. They couldn't tell if it was approaching or receding.

Then it happened.

Big Jim, Whitney, Costaign, Katie, and Pat could only look on in stunned hypnotic trance. What response could they make to the sight of the earth splitting like a putrefied dog! The gulley, beginning at a spot about a hundred yards downhill from them, in answer to the rumbling pressure below, ripped open and roared and lifted, as though a great Krakatoa was lifting its head!

Like a split at the seam, the earth separated. The walls of the water cut were pushed apart, as if by giant hands. In the one blinding second of galactic terror a tide of cockroaches, black, oily, and obscene, bubbled out from the rent! Their insane reproduction had caused such pressure to themselves and the earth that in some spots they geysered into the air. The world was immediately filled with the roar of their presence!

The five stood paralyzed.

The fissure, like fork lighting, streaked up toward them while roaches boiled out from the glutted earth.

So it was really not over at all. Man had killed man, and he thought he had eliminated the only threat. Now the ancient enemy had returned. The undefeated. The

undefeatable. With no malice. No plans. No tactics. N
weapons. Only their massive numbers. And the
insatiable appetites.

Screams from the women brought the men to the
senses. They turned, but there was no place to run.
their panic, Big Jim and Costaign had let go of th
sheriff. They all began to run, blindly, stumblin
scrabbling, tearing, ripping!

"My God!" Costaign screamed. Almost at the sam
time he and Big Jim realized what they had done. The
spun around. Their return motion halted before
began as they saw the sheriff, his mouth wide in th
final shriek of death, his arms flailing over his hea
sliding down into the great earthen maw. Roache
bubbled around him. In an instant, he was gone.

Both men swung around again. They saw, for a brie
second, the women scrambling up the sides of th
gulley. The men did the same.

In a few minutes, they caught up with the womer
Big Jim swung Pat up over his massive shoulder
Together, with the bellowing roar of damnation behine
them, they made one final, desperate dash for life.

The ground suddenly became level. They had reache
the top. There was white water-lapped sand beneath
their feet instead of rocky tan. Before them, the water
of Lake Campbell stretched out serenely, reflecting the
cerulean sky. To their right, the woods thinned out; to
their left, a wide, wooden dam pressed its back agains
the waters. The bellow of doom was still close behine
them.

As soon as they reached the level top, Big Jim and

his terrified burden stumbled and crashed to the ground. Costaign and Katie stopped. All were so exhausted, so frightened, they couldn't speak.

Big Jim, his face flushed, his eyes wide, bathed in sweat, reached into his belt and removed the last two dynamite sticks and the pack of matches. He waved them at Costaign. Big Jim's fiery breath roared in his throat, so that he could barely form words. He waved the sticks toward the dam.

"Base—base," he gasped.

Costaign understood, as the air, like a gradually pitching siren, shrieked louder and louder with the noise of the hellish roaches.

At this point, the gulley was deep and wide. Frantically, Costaign slid down the side. To his left he could see the vanguard of roaches still climbing and swiftly closing in.

He reached the base of the dam. He looked up at the wooden structure towering over him. My God, if I don't get out in time. . . . He held the two sticks in one hand, twining their fuses together. He touched a lit match to them. When they began to fizz, he placed them upright against the base of the wall.

Another mad scramble sent him up the gulley wall. He had barely flung himself over the top when the earth shook beneath him.

He guessed he expected the wall to blast away in a million pieces, as he had seen in the movies, but nothing happened, only a geyser of sand rose lazily into the air.

Big Jim, Katie, and Pat crawled over to join him.

Together they looked over the edge at the undamaged dam. He had failed. There was no life left in their faces; they had run and fought as hard as they could. The four pairs of eyes simply remained glued to the wall in despair as the titanic roar of the roaches got nearer and nearer.

Costaign closed his eyes. And prepared to die. Even that horror was pale beside his great inner discouragement, his failure.

Then another sound. A rending. A creaking. Costaign lifted his head. Beside him, four heads were lifted.

It started as a tiny hole. A trickle of water giggled out. The sound of tearing grew louder. The tiny hole started to split, wider and wider. The trickle became a spurt. The spurt, a jet. A finger of wet earth pointed down the gulley.

Big Jim slapped Costaign on the back. "You did it!" he shouted into the doctor's ear. "You weakened it just enough!"

In the next second, talk was not possible, at any range. Added to the noise of the roaches was the final boom. Millions of tons of water, pressing, pushing, finally smashed the arms that had held them for so long. The dam was washed away. An instant later, the water cut was a white-water river.

In five minutes, the only sound to be heard was the water. The din of the cockroaches was silent at last.

In the dying last rays of the sun, Big Jim and Katie reached County Road 179. They emerged onto the tarmac and sat down to wait for Bob and Pat, still railing behind. For a while, there was silence; each was too heavy with the feeling of loss.

Big Jim slipped his arms around Katie.

"Be kinda tough without John," she said softly.

"Yeah."

Big Jim looked at her. He was not used to traveling alone. I never tried it with a woman though, he thought. Might not be the worst idea in the world. Besides, there's more to life than knocking around and fighting wars. He was getting a little too old for that shit.

Bob still supported Pat as they climbed the last rocks before spotting the flat, open highway a hundred yards ahead. They stumbled to a halt and sucked burning air into their lungs. Slowly, still clinging to each other, they slid to the ground. Bob turned to Pat, who lay face down, panting. Once more he was struck with the fact of her humanity, slowly, like a picture coming into focus. A few mintues ago they had been like animals clawing against a malignant universe. They ran, fought, screamed—without wills, without minds, only with the instinct to stay alive. They were now safe in a friendly darkness though the aura of horror still clung to them.

But Costaign would not think about that now. He was safe, alive. His body and spirit opened and moved out toward the woman next to him, the one who, one day, might be as important as his life.

Pat lifted herself onto her elbows and turned her head slowly to Costaign. In the darkness, her eyes glistened through the dirt, the sweat matted on her face. She reached out and touched him, to assure herself that the figure lying beside her was real.

"We made it," Bob sighed.

She nodded.

They looked deep into each other and knew that soon they would have a lot to say. When they walked away from this they would walk away changed.

"Come on, Pat," he whispered.

Bob leaned over and kissed her tenderly. He was ready for a change and he wanted it to start now.

estselling Excitement from
e International Master of
ction and Suspense.

Alistair
MacLean

FREE
Fawcett Books Listing

There is Romance, Mystery, Suspense, and Adventure waiting for you inside the Fawcett Books Order Form. And it's yours to browse through and use to get all the books you've been wanting . . . but possibly couldn't find in your bookstore.

This easy-to-use order form is divided into categories and contains over 1500 titles by your favorite authors.

So don't delay—take advantage of this special opportunity to increase your reading pleasure.

Just send us your name and address and 35¢ (to help defray postage and handling costs).

FAWCETT BOOKS GROUP
P.O. Box C730, 524 Myrtle Ave., Pratt Station, Brooklyn, N.Y. 11205

Name_____
(please print)

Address_____

City _____ State _____ Zip _____

Do you know someone who enjoys books? Just give us their names and addresses and we'll send them an order form too!

Name_____
Address_____
City_____ State _____ Zip _____

Name_____
Address_____
City_____ State _____ Zip _____